The House on the Shore

Jim O'Malley's Uncle Martin lives in a dilapidated old mansion on the Connemara coast, but when Jim arrives there the house is deserted except for a large black cat and a multitude of spiders. Jim is puzzled by the local people's obvious dislike of his uncle, and the air of mystery surrounding the old man is heightened by the appearance of two strange foreign sailors and Jim's discovery of a cache of guns in a friend's outhouse. A fast-moving succession of strange events leads to an exciting climax, in which Jim and his friend Roddy have to pit their wits against both the foreign intruders and the local community.

Eilís Dillon has written a number of books for children, including *The Lost Island*, also published in Beavers.

D1352106

THE HOUSE ON THE SHORE

Eilís Dillon

Illustrated by Peter Archer

Beaver Books

First published in 1955 by
Faber and Faber Limited
3 Queen Square, London WC1

This paperback edition published in 1977 by
The Hamlyn Publishing Group Limited
London · New York · Sydney · Toronto
Astronaut House, Feltham, Middlesex, England

© Copyright Text Eilís Dillon 1955
ISBN 0 600 34540 8

Printed in England by
Hazell Watson & Viney Limited
Aylesbury, Bucks
Set in Monotype Ehrhardt

Contents

1   I go to Cloghanmore

After a night of heavy rain, I left the hut in which I had sheltered and came down the mountain at last to my uncle's house. The track ran with water, shining cold and clear as if it were already winter. Then the sun rose higher and the light became a soft gold. Little white clouds in a deep blue sky were reflected in the still pools on either side of me. Away down before me the grey-blue sea moved restlessly, as if it were shaking off the purple haze that rolled back and back beyond the horizon as I watched.

I was very hungry, for last night had seen the end of the food I had brought with me from home. The September air put an edge on my appetite, and I hurried down the little path, keeping a sharp eye out for a house where I might have breakfast. Presently the path took a turn, and then I saw the white gable of a cottage huddled against the mountain to my right. A short stony boreen led in to the cottage. There was no gate, and I paused only to observe that a feather of smoke came from the chimney before starting towards it.

The boreen took me to the front door, which looked down towards the sea. The half-door was shut, and I looked over the top of it into the kitchen. A fat old woman in a red petticoat and a plaid head-shawl was stooping over the fire, raking out a red coal and putting a big brown teapot sitting on it. Sweet blue turf-smoke drifted through the room. The kitchen table was under the window by the door, and a white-haired man sat at the head of it, leaning back like a lord waiting for his breakfast. A huge pile of soda-bread was in front of him, and a pat of butter with a cow's head imprinted on it lay on a cabbage-leaf beside the bread. His big earthenware mug had a deep band of blue flowers all round the top. It was so like the scene I knew would be in my kitchen at home at this same hour that I almost imagined myself back again at the other side of the mountain with my journey still before me.

The old man saw me at once. He got up quietly and said:

'Come in, boy, come in. Where did you spring from?'

While I fumbled for the bolt on the inside of the half-door, his wife turned from the fire to look at me, with the brown teapot-lid held high in her hand. Then she came waddling towards me.

'Come on in, agrá. I never laid eyes on you before.' She peered into my face. 'What part of the world are you from?'

'From Borris, Ma'am,' I said. 'Near Newport that is.'

My voice was husky, because I had not used it since the evening before. The old woman lifted her hands with a little shriek, though she kept a tight hold on her teapot-lid.

'Near Newport? And how in the world did you get here?'

'I walked,' said I.

'Over the mountain?' asked the man in his soft voice.

'Yes,' I said, 'I spent last night up there, in a sheep-hut.'

They said I was very brave, and that it was the mercy of God the fairies hadn't got me, or that I hadn't chanced to step on the Hungry Grass. If that had happened, they said, I would not have been able to move a step, and I would have died up there all alone. It sounded very sad, the way they said it. Then the old woman asked me my name. I told her I was called Jim O'Malley, and she nodded wisely:

'Everyone in Newport direction is called O'Malley.'

'Nearly everyone, anyway,' said her husband heartily. 'And hereabouts everyone is called Joyce. My name is Patrick Joyce, and this is my wife Mary, and we're just going to have breakfast and you're going to have it with us, if you're hungry enough.'

I assured him that I was, and we all sat down at the table and worked silently through the pile of soda-bread, and the pat of butter with the cow's head on it. Then we drank the tea-pot dry, and Patrick reached up above the fireplace for his clay pipe and his tin of tobacco.

'And would it be any harm to ask what brings you this way?' he asked as he filled the pipe.

Mrs Joyce leaned her elbows on the table and hitched herself forward in her chair. I could see that she was burning with curiosity. From the way that her husband's quizzical eye rested on her, I guessed with what difficulty she had restrained herself from showering questions on me. It was obvious that she did not often see strangers.

'I'm going to my uncle's house, at Cloghanmore,' I said. 'Am I far from there now?'

'Two miles down the mountain road,' said Patrick, 'then along the coast westwards for another two and you're in Cloghanmore. You'll see the houses and the church, and the quay with pook-awns and nobbies. Oh, they're comfortable people below in Cloghan. There's hardly a man that hasn't his own boat.'

'True for you,' Mrs Joyce cut in impatiently. 'And who is your uncle? Would it be Paddy Conneeley, now, that has the shop, or Scoot Faherty in the forge, or is it one of the boatmen that go to the Aran Islands? Or maybe it's the schoolmaster, even, for you look like a boy that's had a bit of learning.'

'There's a choice of uncles for you!' said Patrick Joyce with a chuckle, but the humour left him suddenly when I said:

'My uncle's name is Martin Walsh.'

They looked at each other quickly, and away again. There was a little silence. Then Patrick cleared his throat loudly and said:

'Ah, yes. I know Martin Walsh.' He fitted the cap firmly on his pipe and asked casually: 'Have you been to visit him before?'

'Never,' I said. 'Didn't I have to ask you the way to Cloghan-more?'

9

'So you had, boy, so you had. And why have you taken it into your head to visit him now?'

It did not occur to me to resent these questions. I was fifteen years old at the time, and at that age a boy will answer almost any question that a grown man cares to ask him.

'My Uncle Martin is my mother's elder brother,' I explained. 'When I was very small he wrote once and asked after me. He said he could do with a strong boy about the place. My mother wrote to him and explained that I was far too young to leave home, but that when I would be older she would send me to him. He never answered that letter. My mother says she thinks he was very angry because I was not older, and he cared so little for any of us that he did not remember how long I was in the world at all.'

'That's like your Uncle Martin, all right,' said Mrs Joyce softly.

I went on hurriedly:

'Still, when I was older she thought of him again. There is not enough work for both myself and my father in our farm. And I think she has an idea that Uncle Martin might take a fancy to me' – I stammered. 'She says he has a big house –'

'Your Uncle Martin doesn't fancy anyone but himself,' said Patrick Joyce firmly. 'If you take my advice you'll go up that mountain again and back to Newport where your own people are. If you make good time you'll be over the top and half-way down the other side before the evening. I'll direct you to a house where you can spend the night. Then, if you got a drive on a cart, maybe, you'll be with your mother by to-morrow night.'

He was so determined about it that I almost got up there and then and started home. But then I remembered my mother's face, and the hopes she had had that I would find my fortune with Uncle Martin. I could not possibly go home without having laid eyes on him at all, just at the word of a stranger. I tried to sound more confident than I felt as I said:

'I can't turn back now. At least I must meet my uncle and

find out for myself what he is like. Besides, he is expecting me.'

'Is he, indeed?' said Patrick easily. 'Did he say so?'

'No,' I mumbled, 'but my mother wrote and said I was coming. Why should I go home again?' I demanded suddenly. 'What sort of a man is my uncle?'

'He's a mean, shifty rasper of a man,' said Patrick calmly. 'He's the sort of man that would take the jacket of a gooseberry. He'd skin a flea for its hide and tallow. You won't hear as much as one good word for him in the whole barony of Cloghanmore.' My heart sank into my boots. 'I wouldn't tell you at all only that you look a decent sort of a lad,' Patrick said, a little more kindly. 'I don't think you have a drop of his watery blood in you. He has the big house and the money, but he has a small, black heart, and he's no good to God or man. It would be better for you not to go next nor near him.'

There was a reputation! But the very fact that it was so bad made me curious to see my uncle, and to find out more about him. There and then I abandoned hope that he would do anything for me.

'As I've come so far, I may as well go the rest of the way,' I said.

Mrs Joyce got up from the table without a word. She lifted the tea-pot off the hearth and went to rinse it by the back door. Patrick stood up too. He was a tall man, and the height of him towering over me made me feel small and weak. Suddenly, too, his face had become hard and unfriendly.

'Then you'd best be going at once,' he said. 'I won't say I'm sorry I gave you your breakfast, for I think there isn't much harm in you. But if you are going down to Cloghanmore House, I'll give you one piece of advice. Don't ask your way of anyone in the village, or you'll maybe find you have more enemies than you can handle.'

I thanked him as best I could and asked him for directions for finding the house. He gave them to me, but neither he nor his wife came to the door to see me go. This was so strange from people of their kind that it made more impression on me than anything they could say. I slipped out of the house, feeling like a ghost, and got back to the mountain path as fast as I could. At the end of the boreen I looked back, remembering my joy at my first sight of Patrick Joyce's cottage. It looked very different to me now.

Still, with the sun shining, and the bright sea glittering below, my spirits revived as I continued on my way. Soon I began to pass other houses, where silent dogs, fat from breakfast, came out to lie in the sun with no more than a sleepy eye for me. The women were too busy feeding the hens or washing up the breakfast mugs to have time to follow and question me, and the men were still indoors enjoying their pipes, I supposed, for they were not yet on their way to work. I was very pleased at this, for I was determined to take at least one piece of Patrick Joyce's advice. If I had to ramble around Cloghanmore all day, I would not again ask my way to my uncle's house.

After a while the track became a road, and great ricks of good black turf were piled on either side of it, ready for the carts to take them into Galway to be sold. Then I saw Cloghanmore village. Its one street curved round a tiny semicircular bay. A long quay stretched out into the sea, and sheltered the village from storms. The water was still and black and shiny at the lee side of the quay, and several fishing boats were tied up there. While I watched, others came sliding silently in from the sea, until they were three deep along the quay wall. They were all freshly tarred and their sails were new and strong. As I came closer I could see the new fish boxes and lobster pots piled on their little decks and the new nets and gear. Altogether, I had never seen such a prosperous-looking fleet of boats.

I did not go down to the quay when I reached the village. The men would be tired after their night's fishing, I knew, but for all that they might take too much interest in me. I marched along the street as if I knew exactly where I was going, and though people looked at me curiously, no one tried to stop me.

Out of the tail of my eye I saw a shop with 'P. Conneeley. Grocer and Vintner' over the door. This would be the Paddy Conneeley that Mrs Joyce had mentioned. I passed the forge, too, at the end of the street, and saw the blacksmith in the depths of it, shoeing a huge white horse. I wondered why he was called 'Scoot' Faherty, but this was not the time to stop and find out.

After the forge the houses were more scattered. The road turned a little inland now, but I could hear the sea only one field away, on my left. It was a flat, soft field, and looked sour, as if the sea came in and took possession of it for a few months every winter. Up on my right-hand side the mountain stretched to the sky. It was not rocky there, but covered with a sedgy grass and streaked at the top with silver lines where the little streams still ran down after the night's rain.

Half a mile beyond the village, I saw the woods of Cloghanmore House. I knew them at once, for Patrick Joyce had told me they were the only trees in the district. They were on the sea side of the road, tall old beeches and chestnuts, now turning a rich orange, and shining with a misty beauty under the morning sun. I felt a strange tingling run all over me as if I had suddenly crossed the border into the land of youth, and might at any moment meet a company of beautiful unearthly people on horseback, riding to some fairy battle. I remember standing in the middle of the road in a sort of trance, expecting I don't know what wild adventure to begin. But it was an old yellow nanny-goat grazing on the ditch that brought me to myself. She left her perch and came over to me, munching busily, while her long beard wagged. I rubbed her forehead and looked into her odd, yellow eyes that almost matched her long fur. Then I led her back to the grassy margin of the road and lay down to rest, while she cropped the grass all around me in short, crisp bites.

A little farther along the road I could see double iron gates opening on to an avenue of trees. This was the way for a welcome guest to visit my Uncle Martin, without a doubt. But I did not think it was the best way for me. To tell the truth, I was

13

both afraid and ashamed of my uncle, and I did not want to run the risk of being turned away from his door. Patrick Joyce had made it clear that my uncle was hated by the entire neighbourhood, and until I knew what was behind this feud I was determined to go very cautiously.

So I made up my mind to approach his house from the shore, and to be ready to retreat the same way if I did not like my reception.

Near me where I lay, a grassy lane led between two stone walls towards the sea. I followed it for a piece, and found that it ended at a well, paved at the edges with flat stones. The nanny-goat had come with me, and I thought she sniggered when I lay down and had a long drink, like a cow. But when I looked quickly up at her, she seemed quite solemn, so that I could not accuse her.

A little stream ran out of the well, between low bramble-covered banks. I stepped into it, in my bare feet, to use it as a path to the shore. The goat bleated in mockery, and turned back to the main road again.

It was not far to the shore by my watery path. It was a rough shore, all covered with big round stones, worn smooth by the winter seas. I walked along the top, where there was a little grass, until I was at the edge of the woods. Now, I could see how the trees were all blown away from the sea, and the outer line of them withered with the salt spray. The wind, which I had hardly noticed before, sang a high sad song in the branches. I climbed a low stone wall, dropped on to a soft warm carpet of last year's leaves and walked into the wood. There was no path here, and I followed at random the direction in which I thought the house would be. Wet branches trailed across the ground and caught at my legs. Above me the leaves almost shut out the daylight. I could hear wood-pigeons and blackbirds up there, angry at my approach. The nearer I came to the house the more dense became the wood, with snowberry bushes and yew trees interspersed with the bigger trees. The yews gave me a lot of

15

trouble, because their strong branches grew straight out from the trunks almost at ground level, and made the way quite impassable at times, so that I had to make long detours to avoid them. Only at one place I found a little clearing, where some grass grew, and soft moss climbed a short distance up the trunks of the trees. At one corner of this clearing there was a little path, so faint that it could hardly be called a path at all. I had only followed it for a few yards, when it took a sudden twist and brought me out at the edge of the wood, a stone's throw from the house.

It had once been a fine house, as I could see by its broad windows and handsome stone steps. But it was in a sad state of repair now, with patches of raw cement on its once yellow walls, and wisps of ivy hanging down from the very roof. Broken slates from the roof lay on the ground at my feet. I wondered if they had ever been replaced. It was all as still and as silent as a mountain graveyard. Not even the birds stirred here.

A patch of rough grass stretched between me and the side wall of the house, where I stood gaping, half hidden, still in the bushes. I came forward slowly and walked around to the weedy gravel sweep in front of the main door. Two spiritless stone lions, overgrown with moss, sat on pedestals at either side of the steps. One had had his nose newly knocked off, but he still stared ahead quite unconcerned. I was surprised to find the old studded door standing open.

Here was some sign of life at last, I thought. An open door is always a cheerful sight. I ran up the steps and lifted the old black knocker, and hammered loudly with it. The knocker was a ring in the nose of yet another sheepish-looking lion. No one came. I hammered again, and this time I waited for no more than a minute before stepping into the long hall.

It was an eerie place. The floor was made of uneven flagstones, none too clean, and at the far end another huge door led, I supposed, into the kitchen quarters. Suddenly I called out:

'Is there anyone there?'

For the answer came a faint 'Miaow!' from the half-open door on my left, but no human voice. I pushed the door open boldly and walked into the room. It was flagged also and looked out towards the front of the house. There were musty leather chairs and an ancient table, black with smoke and age, in the middle of the room. The curtains were black too, and had once had a design of cranes in flight on them, but now they hung in ribbons. There was an immense fireplace in rough-cut limestone on the wall opposite the windows, and the remains of a very small fire of turf smouldered on its huge hearth. A stout black cat sat on the hearth too, as near the fire as he dared to go without singeing his valuable coat. He half-turned a disdainful eye on me, as if I were an old acquaintance, and repeated his casual 'Miaow'.

'Miaow, yourself,' said I. 'I'm very glad to see you. Where there's a cat and a fire there's human life of some kind.'

And I left the dismal room more cheerfully than I had entered it. At the far end of the hall I looked for the kitchen, and found it at the end of another passageway. It was flagged too, and its whitewash had not been renewed for years. Against one wall was a rickety old red dresser with cracked mugs and bowls, and a few blue and white plates. The ceiling was covered with hooks for bacon, but not as much as an ounce of it hung up there. There were spiders in plenty, though, running and pausing and running again. I was sure they were watching me, and making ill-bred remarks about my appearance. In one corner a rheumaticky old fellow, as big as a sparrow, crawled out an inch from his perch to stare, and then shuffled back again, having seen, I supposed, that I was not good to eat.

There was an open fire here too, almost smothered in ashes. Desolate pots were ranged on either side, and a dusty iron kettle hung from the crane. I lifted the lid and found it half-full of lukewarm water. I turned back to the smoke-blackened kitchen table, and then I stopped suddenly. Lying on the table was the letter that my mother had written announcing my coming. I picked it up slowly and read it. Yes, she had given the right day

17

and hour of my arrival. And here was my welcome! It almost looked, I thought angrily, as if my uncle had deserted his house rather than meet me.

Again I had to make up my mind that I was not going to crawl away tamely. I would sit down right here in my uncle's kitchen and wait for him to come home. And I would wait in comfort too. I seized the big turf basket that stood empty beside the fire, tipped a family of spiders out of it on to the floor, marched to the back door and flung it open. There was a cobbled yard out there, all surrounded with coach-houses and sheds of all kinds. I saw the open turf-shed, and went across to fill my basket. Through the wide doorway of a coach-house nearby I could see the fresh wheel-marks of a trap on the sandy floor. As I walked back carrying the heavy basket I passed an open stable with hay in the manger and straw on the floor, but no horse. Some of my anger lessened, as it occurred to me that my uncle might have had to go a distance in his pony-trap and been de-layed in his return. But I did not set much store by this idea, for I had already observed that Cloghanmore House was indeed the house of a miser, and that all Patrick Joyce had told me about my uncle seemed to be true. More than anything it hurt me that my uncle knew I was coming and was not there to welcome me. The meanest of welcomes would have served, I thought.

I built a wall of turf across the back of the hearth, raked out the fire and put the red part in the middle, and surrounded it with more turf. Then I fanned it with my cap until a little flame sprang up.

The only sign of comfort in the kitchen was a big grand-mother's chair with cushions, standing against the wall. Now I pulled this out, arranged it to my satisfaction in front of the fire and sat down in it. The spiders scurried and scuttled and whispered at my boldness but I cared nothing for them. I lay back and closed my eyes. And because I had walked through two counties, and had spent two wet nights on the road and had met such a cold reception at the end of it, I was so tired within and without that in less than a minute I was fast asleep.

2 Pietro and Miguel

When I awoke it was dusk. I was stiff from sleeping in the big chair, and very cold. I looked in astonishment at the remains of the fire that I had built. It had crumbled down to a heap of brown ash. I must have been asleep for hours. The kitchen window looked out to the side of the house, and it seemed to me that the dark trees out there had moved closer. It would have been easy for me to believe that they were full of pookas and other malignant spirits, all watching me through the uncurtained glass. I tried to laugh at such foolishness but with all my heart I wished that I could shut out the staring night.

The first thing to be done was to make up the fire. I did this, using all the remaining turf in the basket, and was soon rewarded with a comforting little flame that partly lit up the dark room. Then, leaving the back door open, I brought the basket out into the yard and refilled it. I took time to listen at the stable door for the rustle of a horse's hooves in the straw, but it was all still and empty in there. I came back to the kitchen very down-hearted.

I was cruelly hungry again, and this with the cold that had awakened me took all the spirit out of me. I wanted to explore my uncle's grounds a little more before it would become completely dark, but I knew I would not have the courage to face even a bat if I went out hungry as I was. There was but one cupboard in the kitchen, and I guessed that the food would be kept there. I hoped that my uncle would not return to find me ransacking the cupboard, but I determined to make no apology if he did.

Alas, there was little enough to ransack. Part of a stale loaf of soda-bread and a lump of raw bacon the size of an onion were all that I found. Nearby on the bare shelf there was a can half-full of stale beer, with a spider drowned in it, all pickled by the alcohol. In a drawer of the kitchen table I found a fork with which to fish him out. With the same fork I held the bacon close to the fire until it was cooked. The ashes flew up softly on it so that it was like eating a small wet sod of turf. The bread had grown a short beard, a faint blue in colour. I reminded myself that this was healthy stuff, very good, as I knew, for curing a cut finger, and sent it down after the bacon. It was very dry, and I turned a doubtful eye on the can of beer. The drowned spider was the trouble there, but at last I poured some into a cracked mug off the dresser, closed my eyes and tasted it. I found it very pleasant. Perhaps the spider had given it a special flavour. I have often drunk beer since then, but never any I liked as well as that first mugful. It sent a little fire racing up and down my veins, and gave me back a little of my courage.

In the dresser drawer I found an old candle with tooth-marks where the mice had been nibbling at it. I lit it at the fire and placed it on the window-sill. Its little yellow face looked back at it, reflected in the glass, and its light cast huge gloomy shadows around the room. Now I could hear the wind crying and moaning around the house, and for a moment I felt like joining in. At home I had never feared the dark. In the evening our lighted open door could be seen a mile away, and my mother moving about the kitchen made the whole house feel warm and secure with her presence. But ours was a little house, not in the least like this great eerie barrack where an army could lurk undetected.

I opened the back door. It was lighter than it had seemed from within. There was a watery moon, and I thought it would come on to rain later. I chose to come out this way, for I did not fancy feeling my way through the dark house. Down beyond the turf-house I had noticed a wooden gate leading out of the yard, and when I reached it I was pleased to find it was not locked. At the side of the gate the trees began again, with a tiny path running alongside them. I followed the path until it left the trees behind and started to go down towards the sea. I could hear waves dragging on shingle. A moment later I caught the shine of breakers glittering in the moonlight. It seemed that this was my uncle's private way to the sea, and I wondered if I might at last find some sign of his whereabouts.

It was a stony beach, as I had guessed from the sound of the waves. Two reefs about a quarter of a mile apart formed a sort of bay, and in between a short slip had been built out into the sea. I thought the beach must shelve sharply here, because in the half-light I could see that the water at the end of the slip was dark, and that the waves did not begin to break until they were almost ashore. And tied up at the end of the slip was a boat, with a lighted lantern hanging on its bows.

I was standing at the end of the path from the house while I observed all this. The path finished here, and now the top of the beach was the only road. On my right there were fields with loose stone walls, and on my left a grassy bank that ended in low cliffs. I moved closer to the wall the better to see the boat, and then my heart jumped so that I thought it must have knocked against my teeth. I stood as still as a pointing dog and listened.

On the other side of the wall I could hear a low-voiced conversation in Irish. There were two people there. After a moment I realised that they were quite unaware of my presence. They were too busy watching the boat through holes in the wall that faced the sea. At first I thought of calling out to them and asking if they had seen my uncle, but the next moment the words shrivelled up in my throat. One voice had said, low and eager:

'With my good knife I'll finish off the small one while you attend to the other.'

'No, no!' said the second voice. 'That is not the way to do it. We must all work together and capture them, and hand them over to the Guards.'

'The Guards!' said the first voice contemptuously. 'The Guards will only tell them to be good boys in future and let them off again. We can't prove anything against them.'

'True for you,' said the other. 'But I don't want any business with knives all the same. Put that knife into your pocket this minute, Roddy. I know you have it there in your hand.'

'Oh, all right,' said the one called Roddy sulkily. 'But if we wait too long we'll maybe not get a chance at them at all.'

'We won't wait that long,' said the other grimly.

There was a pause, during which it occurred to me that I myself might be 'the small one' that was to be finished off with a knife, and my uncle the other one. For all I knew this blood-thirsty pair had observed my arrival at the house, and thought that I had come to help my uncle out of his difficulties, whatever they might be. At that moment I wished I had taken Patrick Joyce's advice, and had gone back to Borris, where we don't carry knives with which to attack innocent strangers.

I had less than a minute for this useless wish before I got my second surprise. Two figures were moving about down by the boat. I saw them for a moment against the last streak of light above the sea. Then they started to walk up the slip. I could hear the heavy thump of seaboots. Now I was in a fix. I did not know whether to run and risk pursuit by the watchers behind the wall, or to stay and talk with the men off the boat. It looked like one of the Connemara boats, though I could not see properly at this distance, and there was nothing secretive about the way that the lamp was hung from the bows. Perhaps one of these men was my uncle, coming home at last. A moment later, as the two men stepped off the slip on to the grass, I saw that one of them was very small. Probably this was 'the small one', and not myself, I thought, and I felt mighty relieved. I shrank back into the shadows, trying to look like part of the stone wall. I would wait until the men had reached me before stepping out boldly and introducing myself. They were not troubling to go quietly. And why should my uncle come sneaking back to his own house,

I thought, like a thief or a coward?

But as they came close to me, the big man paused to put a match to his pipe. In the little light I saw a heavy dark face, with a hooked nose, and – my mouth opened at the sight – long greasy black hair in curls down to his shoulders. This was no Irishman. I wondered for a moment if the little man could be my uncle, but as they passed me he sang a few bars of a song in a foreign language, and was abruptly silenced by the other. Though I did not understand the language, it was easy to hear the note of warning in the big man's voice. Then they passed me quite close, without suspecting my presence.

My knees were shaky now, and I would have liked to sit down. But first I had to wait while my two neighbours behind the wall had another chat. Roddy was lamenting at the grand opportunity that he had missed and his companion was soothing him, and seemed to be regretting his own caution.

I leaned against the wall to wonder what it was all about, what kind of battlefield had I encountered, and what country had produced the extraordinary-looking pair who had started off so confidently for my uncle's house. This was not their first visit, I could see. Even in the dusk they had had no difficulty in finding their way to the path beside the wood. And my candle, set in the window, would guide them straight to the kitchen door.

Now there were sounds of movement behind the wall, and then I realised that my neighbours were going away. I stretched upwards and looked over the top, but it was very dark, and I could only see two dark shapes that moved up the field and faded into the blackness. Now, with even my fear gone, I felt very lonesome.

A sudden puff of wind carrying a few heavy drops of rain brought me to myself again. I ran along the grass and down to the boat-slip, hoping that the men would not change their minds and come back before I would have had time to examine the boat. The wet flags were slippery with sea-weed, for the tide was not yet full in, and I had to pick my steps carefully for the last part of the way.

Before I reached the boat I knew by the shape of her that she was a Connemara hooker. The thin moonlight shone on her tarred sides and silvered her mast and sheets. I lay on my stomach on the wet stones and read her name by the light of the moon. She was called *Saint Brendan*, and she looked fit to sail the Atlantic as Saint Brendan the Navigator did, in just such a boat as this.

But what were the two foreigners doing on an Irish hooker, I wondered. Suddenly the horrid thought occurred to me that the owner of the boat could be aboard her now, watching me from the dark square of the hold. I lay as still as a rabbit when the weasel's eye is on him, but the only sound I could hear was the chuckle of the black water between the boat and the slip, and the heavy sweep of the wind high above me. I got away from that boat like a snake slipping through the jungle, crawling close to the ground until I reached the top of the slip. Then I got up on my legs and bolted for the path. I looked back once to see if a huge figure were pounding after me, but only the moon looked down curiously at me from among stormy clouds.

When I reached the path I went more cautiously. I had taken a great dislike to the open places, where people whispered about knives behind walls, and a great snag-toothed giant lurked in the hold of a boat waiting to bite the head off any innocent passer-by. I was determined to barricade myself into my uncle's house until morning, and to start for home with the first light of day. I had had enough excitement to last me for many a year to come.

I decided to go to the front door, and I followed the path that went along by the side of the house. As I passed the kitchen window I saw that my candle was no longer lighting. Perhaps it was burned out, I thought, for I had surely been nearly an hour away. I kept close to the house until I reached the corner, and waited there with my heart pounding, and listened. It was all perfectly still except for the sighing of the great trees. I supposed that the two visitors, finding the house deserted, must have walked on to the village to have a drink and a chat with the people, as the foreign fishermen always did.

But when I reached the front door it was shut fast. I pushed at it with all my strength, but I might as well have been pushing at the stone wall beside it. I ran back by the way that I had come, and found that the door into the yard was open. But the kitchen door was locked, and through the small window beside it I could see the tantalising glow of my fire.

With my hand raised to hammer on the door I paused. It was my own fault that I was shut out, for I should have sat tight by that fire and waited for my uncle to come home. Perhaps he was in there now, entertaining his guests with the rest of the can of beer and the few crumbs of mouldy bread that I had left lying on the table.

It was the thought of that meal that sent me away from the house again. If my uncle was as churlish as the state of his larder seemed to show, then I was in no hurry to seek his company. I turned away from the door, rejecting the temptation to give it a resounding kick.

At first I was at a loss where to spend the night. The stable was there, warm and inviting, and still empty. I had slept in stables before, and had always found them cheerful places, full of the smell of leather and horses. There were other sheds too, and a sleepy hen yawned in one of them while I stood there hesitating. But hens are uncomfortable creatures, and in any case I did not fancy accepting hospitality from them when I had been refused it by my uncle. I could return to Patrick Joyce's house, to be sure, and would probably be given a bed and a welcome even at this late hour. But I did not want to see him again so soon, and to have to admit that my uncle had shut me out. Neither did I wish to ask any of the local people to take me in, for they would certainly want to know all about me in return.

It was then that I remembered the little clearing in the wood through which I had passed earlier in the day. It was late in the year for sleeping out, but the trees grew so closely there that I would be certain to find shelter under the interlaced branches. I would make a nest in the fallen leaves and sit there until morning.

I found the way into the wood easily enough, and was instantly plunged into darkness. Still it was easy to keep to the little path, for each time I tried to leave it, the sharp finger of a bush poked me back again. I groped my way thus until I saw a shaft of moonlight ahead of me. A moment later I reached the clearing. I was filled with a soft, eerie light that turned the thin grass a strange colour. I looked around at the ring of tree-trunks, and shivered as much with uneasiness as with the cold of the wind. A few heavy drops of rain fell with a little patter. If my mother could only see me now, I thought longingly. I remembered especially how she used to put hot bricks in my bed to warm it, if I were out late after sheep. But it was no use thinking of this now. My best plan was to find a place to sleep, for I knew that my state would not look so grim in the morning.

I chose a big chestnut tree whose roots stretched out like legs, making a comfortable hollow between where I would be sheltered from the wind. Its big fan-shaped leaves were falling, but a stout stem of ivy had climbed the trunk and had spread a thick mass of twisted branches and leaves up there, making a roof as close as any thatched roof in Connemara. I got into the hollow between the roots and looked upward, and I could not see as much as a speck of sky. If it were not for the mean little wind that crept around me, I should be quite comfortable here.

I lay back against the tree-trunk and closed my eyes. But it was knobbly behind my shoulders, and I could not find an easy position. I sat up again, and then a little scream came up in my throat.

There, dangling a few feet from my nose, was the end of a rope ladder. There was no mistaking it. It was clearly outlined against the faint light from the moon. It swung gently back and forth, and while I watched with my mouth agape it gave a little twitch or jump. Now I could not have screamed or called out to

save my life. I held my breath until I thought my lungs would burst. There was someone at the top of that ladder, I was certain. I had a wild hope that whoever it was did not know of my presence. I began to edge out of my hollow, thinking to crawl away through the undergrowth. But when I stood up at the foot of the tree I could not resist looking upward, to see where the ladder came from.

There, looking down at me, was a head. It was cocked on one side, like the head of a huge bird, so that the eyes gleamed dully in the moonlight. This is how I sometimes see it still in my dreams, as if there were no body, but only that face like a wrinkled chestnut long forgotten in a drawer. We stared at each other for almost a minute, and then there came a dry little laugh and a cracked voice, like an old woman's, said:

'I'm afraid I frightened you.'

I recovered my breath all at once to shout:

'You certainly did!'

The voice began to twitter and the queer little head to bob from side to side.

'Oh, do be quiet! Please be quiet! I'm sorry I frightened you. I had to let down the ladder, so that you can come up.'

'Why should I come up?' I asked, but in a lower tone. 'Who are you? For all I know you're waiting your chance to make an end of me.'

'No, no! I won't injure you,' said the voice. 'You are Jim O'Malley, aren't you!'

'That is my name,' I said. 'But I don't know how you know it.'

'Of course I know it,' said the voice querulously. 'Amn't I your Uncle Martin?'

I said no other word, but silently climbed the ladder into the tree.

3   The house in the tree

I had never climbed a rope ladder before. It seemed to give in every direction with my weight, and it swung away under me with each rung that I climbed. And there was my uncle twittering and wailing, and almost weeping to me to be quiet. By the time I had reached the top I was so irritated that I would gladly have pitched him head foremost down to the ground.

The ladder was about ten feet long and it was tied securely to two strong branches of the tree. A kind of platform was built there, and my uncle quickly seized the ladder and pulled it up out of sight. Then he went down on his hands and knees and looked back over his shoulder at me like a playful dog.

'Follow me,' he said, and again I heard his dry little laugh.

I was convinced by now that he was touched in the head, as we say, but he was so small and feeble-looking that I did not feel unsafe with him. I knew that I could hold my own against him if he attacked me, though he had given no sign of doing so. In the faint light I saw him crawl quickly through an opening among the densely growing ivy-leaves, and I went down on all fours and followed suit. In complete darkness I heard him rustle about like a rat, and then all at once he struck a light.

It would be hard to describe the expression on his face as he stood there, holding a candle high and grinning with delight and pride at my astonishment. We were in a little room, about eight feet square, and with a low vaulted roof of thatch. A straw mat hung over the entrance, the same kind of close-plaited mat that the country people use to seal the door against winter

31

draughts. I knew that not a speck of light would show through it. In spite of all the rain that had fallen last night, the ceiling was quite dry. Outside I could hear rain falling again, pattering on the leaves all around us, while the wind swayed the trees and rocked the little house from side to side.

'Well, what do you think of my house?' asked my uncle at last, impatient at my silence. He did not wait for an answer but hurried on excitedly. 'I built it all myself, during the summer. That's hay on the floor, to make it warm. It's laid on branches, all woven in and out. And I pulled down branches and tied them, and thatched them over with straw to make the roof. See my straw mat, for a door? Isn't that clever? Keeps out the draughts.'

'Why must you live up here, crouched like a rat in a hole?' I said.

He was deeply offended.

'It's not in the least like a rat-hole,' he said. 'I spent a lot of time on it.' He poked at me eagerly with his fingers, and his good humour seemed to return. 'You're the first person to see it, you know. Look, I even have some books to read.'

They were there in a corner, in an old wooden box.

'But why must you live in a tree?' I asked again.

Still he avoided answering that question.

'I have a good bed. And one for you too, boy. You can see, I thought of everything.'

He set the candle down on top of the box of books, and I noticed that he was careful to keep the flame well away from the thatch. Perhaps he was not so odd after all, I thought. He stood there now, shifting from one foot to the other with a little shuffle, rubbing his hands.

'Come, now,' he said persuasively. 'What do you think of it?'

Though I did not wish to encourage him, I could not conceal my admiration. I had often dreamed of building a house in a tree, and of making a rope ladder with which to climb up and down to it. I envied my uncle the fun he must have had. I was a bit old for my years at that time, and I remember being surprised that an old man could enjoy such things at all. I said grudgingly:

'It seems to be dry and warm, at any rate.'

That started him off again, and he had to show me how he had used the matted ivy stems as a framework for the roof, and had woven the straw and sods of the thatch in and out from the inner side, so that they should not be seen by anyone passing below.

'I walked through the clearing this morning,' I said, 'and I didn't notice anything unusual.'

'I saw you,' said my uncle with a little squeak of laughter. 'I was watching you from up here. I thought you would never come back.'

'It was only a chance that I did,' I said.

He was not listening to me. He had picked up the candle again, and was holding it close to my face so that he could peer at me.

'You're a well-spoken boy,' he said after a moment. 'What did your mother tell you about me?'

'Not very much,' I said. 'She doesn't talk much about her life in this place.'

I had hoped that I would be able to prod him into telling me something of himself, and of how my mother had come to marry a poor countryman with a wet farm of forty mountainy acres. I could see that Uncle Martin's house had once been comfortable and well furnished, and that the family had been much more prosperous than is usual in that part of the country. I had long ago observed that my mother's way of cooking and housekeeping was different from that of her neighbours, and that ours was the only house, except for the priest's and the schoolteacher's, where there were several shelves of books. But I soon saw that I would get no explanations here. A satisfied look came over my uncle's face, and he turned away to put the candle down again.

'She's a wise woman, your mother,' he said. 'Most of the harm in the world is done by talk. She made a good hand of you, too. I thought you might be a rough, lumpish fellow, like your father.'

'My father doesn't have to roost in a tree, like a turkey-cock,' I said hotly, 'and I never heard that his neighbours talk about him the way yours talk about you!'

I started for the door, and I think I would have left him then in a temper, if he had not laid hold of my arm. His fingers were like the claws of an old turkey-cock, indeed, and I paused to observe with amusement how right I had been in my comparison. He saw my expression soften and seized his advantage eagerly.

'Come, now, we won't be so hasty,' he said. 'You and I are going to be friends. I didn't mean what I said about your father. We won't talk about that sort of thing any more.'

I saw that what he had said was so far from the truth that it would have been a waste of time to have resented it. My father was a quiet, gentle man, who did not speak much, but whose wisdom was deep and sustaining and sure. Outwardly it seemed that my mother was the stronger of the two, but in fact she deferred to him in every important decision. She had more education from books, but he had it from life and from many generations of proud and independent ancestors. To call him lumpish or rough was the purest nonsense. I said as much, and Uncle Martin said:

'Yes, yes. I told you I didn't mean it. Your father didn't like me and I didn't like him, so there was no love lost.'

I could well believe this. I could imagine my father tolerantly summing up Martin Walsh's character and then dismissing him from his mind. Now I remembered how cool my father had been about my prospects in Cloghanmore, and how he had said it would be good for me to learn that everyone was not as honest as our neighbours in Borris. My uncle was watching me anxiously with his head on one side, to see if I were still offended.

'You're quite right,' I said. 'We won't talk about that sort of thing any more.'

'Good, good!' The turkey-claw gripped me again. 'Have you been in the house?'

'Yes, I was there,' I said guardedly. 'I spent the day there.'

'Did you, now? Did you indeed?' he said eagerly.

For the first time I noticed that he was wearing a very old black suit which may have fitted him once, but which now hung in folds around him. He was a very small man, and he was so thin that he looked like a little bundle of bones. He let go of my arm, and his restless hands kept stroking each other and twitching in and out.

'And what did you see in the house?'

'Nothing but the cat,' I said shortly.

'Fursey!' said Uncle Martin. 'Where was he? Did you feed him? Did he look well?'

'Very well,' said I sardonically. 'He was sitting in front of the drawing-room fire.'

'Did you feed him?' he insisted.

'There was nothing to feed him on,' I pointed out. 'There wasn't enough for myself, not to mind an old cat that could go out and catch a rabbit for himself if he felt hungry.'

'Fursey likes his meat cooked,' said Uncle Martin stiffly.

'So do I,' I said hotly, 'and I don't fancy toasting nasty little bits of bacon in the ashes of a turf fire. That's the queerest hospitality I ever got in my life.'

'Please, let us not fall out,' said my uncle. 'I should have left some food for you. But I thought I would be able to get down during the day. Perhaps Fursey did catch a rabbit.' He sighed. 'I brought him here, but he went away again. I'd have thought a cat would like living in a tree. So he was sitting in the drawing-room? Did you sit there too?'

'I favoured the kitchen,' I said, wondering why he watched me so closely. 'I made up the fire and went to sleep in front of it. . . .' I broke off as a thought struck me. 'Who made up the fires this morning? Both fires were well alight, though they were small.'

'I made them up, because I knew you were coming,' said

35

Uncle Martin. 'I slipped down early, while the coast was clear, and did it.'

'While the coast was clear? What is happening here? Why are you not able to live in your own house?'

'I'll explain it all later on,' he said soothingly. 'You must be hungry. We'll have something to eat. You'll see that I'm quite a good cook.'

He was fluttering and giggling again, like a skittish hen, so that it was no use trying to force him to answer my questions. He pulled out a long tin trunk which had stood against one wall, and opened the lid. Inside he had several little spirit stoves and small pots, and as he bent over them preparing the meal he looked like an aged wizard concocting spells. He made me see that the straw mat was fitted tightly over the door, and then he lifted up a hinged flap in the ceiling, to let out the smells, he said. He had a duck, ready plucked, and he cooked her in tomato sauce and onions. He handled the pots as deftly as a woman, and before long an intoxicating smell filled the little house. It was so delicious that I could hardly contain myself until the duck was ready, and I occupied myself with getting out knives and forks and laying the table at my uncle's directions. He was quite particular about warming the plates, but he did not seem to notice that they were none too clean. I said nothing about this either, lest the washing of them might postpone our meal by as much as a minute.

At last we sat down on the soft floor, at either side of the box that served us as a table, and shared the duck between us. My uncle got more than I did, because after he had served me, he took a fancy to a tasty bit on my plate, and took it away from me. Then he sat there munching and looking pleased with himself, and obviously congratulating himself on his cleverness. I made sure to finish my share quickly, so that the same should not happen again.

Presently we had done, and we laid down our knives and forks in silence. My uncle sighed.

'That was a good little duck,' he said. 'I used to call her Maria. I'll miss her a great deal. She used to come running to me when I called her.' He laughed slyly. 'She came once too often.'

'She was a fool to trust you,' I said, and I determined to learn a lesson from her fate.

'Ah, yes, poor little Maria!' said the old scoundrel, shaking his head sentimentally. He reached out a hand for one of her bones and picked it delicately with his long yellow teeth.

I stood up, and began to clear away the plates and cutlery that we had used. Behind me my uncle said suddenly:

'So you spent the whole day in the kitchen?'

'Yes. I fell asleep, in front of the fire.'

'So that anyone who liked could walk about the place, and you'd never have heard them.'

'That's so,' I said. 'I thought you would be home at any moment. I looked in the yard, and when I saw that the horse and trap were gone, I said to myself – '

'The horse and trap gone? Are my horse and trap gone?'

'They're not there now, at any rate,' I began, but he interrupted me with a stream of vile wishes for all the people of Cloghanmore, all in a low, hissing whisper, for he was still careful to make no noise.

At last he fell silent and sat there brooding. I left him to re-open the conversation himself, but he seemed to have forgotten me. I went on with tidying away the plates, trying to look unconcerned. Presently he said, half to himself:

'Yes, you have come just in time. So they took away my horse and trap. . . .'

I said casually:

'You have visitors at the house now.'

Instantly he was on his feet, clutching me.

'Who is at the house? Why didn't you tell me before?'

'I thought you knew about them,' I said. 'Let go of my arm, or I won't tell you at all!'

He sat down again and looked at me, but he was finding it hard to be friendly now, as I could see. The candlelight shone on the tight, yellow skin of his nose, making it look like a beak.

'They came off a boat called *Saint Brendan*,' I said.

'Yes, yes. My own boat,' he nodded eagerly.

'There are two of them, one big and one small,' I continued. 'I saw them land and go up the path to the house. The big fellow's hair grows down to his shoulders, like a girl's.'

He did not show any surprise at this, so I guessed that he was well acquainted with his visitors.

'When I got back to the house the doors were shut,' I finished, 'and I'm sure the two of them are within.'

'Of course, of course!' said Uncle Martin impatiently. 'They know they are welcome. Did they ask you about me?'

'They didn't see me at all,' I said. 'And they looked so queer that I kept out of their way.'

'Did you not knock on the door?'

'No. I had no reason to believe that I would be welcome.'

He made a little impatient sound, and then sat there, thumping one hand into the other while his face twitched with a mixture of fear and cunning that was most unpleasant to watch.

'So they are in the house, alone,' he said. 'I don't like that. That won't do at all. I must go down to them. Yes, I must go down.' Suddenly he looked up at me sideways. 'No, you'll go. That will be much better. Yes, you're young and lively, and you can find out what's happening, and run back here at once and tell me. Don't let them catch you, though. I don't want them to know you're here just yet.'

You may be sure I did not like the sound of this. I could imagine that if they did catch me, Uncle Martin would make a few regretful remarks about me in the same tone that he had used about Maria, the duck. Then he would smirk to himself in a pleased way, because he himself was safe, and forget me. Still I did not at once refuse to go. I was tired of being cooped up in the house in the tree, and I was also wildly curious to know what scoundrelly tricks my uncle was at. He had showed no sign of answering my questions, and I could see that he had no intention of doing so. It seemed to me that the only way for me to discover the answers was to go back to the house and try to overhear the conversation of the two men. Suddenly a difficulty occurred to me, and I asked:

'Where do your visitors come from?'

'The big fellow is an Italian, and the other is from South America,' he said blandly, grinning at me.

'Do they speak English?'

'They speak some strange language of their own – maybe it's an Italian dialect, maybe it's some kind of sailor's language. I don't know.'

And he pretended to examine his finger-nails, while he could not help looking upwards at me under his eyebrows, and shaking with amusement at my predicament. I said carelessly:

'Then I won't be able to understand what they are saying, even if I get close enough to overhear them.'

'That's true,' he said, and laughed outright.

'Then what can I learn by going down to look at them?' I said.

'You can see which room they are sitting in, and what they are doing there. That will be very important, especially if' – he paused, as if he were afraid of giving away too much information. Then he went on with a little rush: 'Especially if they are in the drawing-room!' And he clapped his hand over his mouth and looked at me over the fingers with staring eyes.

This was not the first time that he had shown his interest in the drawing-room. I wondered what the reason could be, and remembered the great cold room with the age-blackened table and mouldy chairs. It would be hard to hide a mystery in that room. I said:

'If they are in the drawing-room, I'll be able to see them, but the kitchen windows are too high.'

'Surely you can climb up to look in,' he said eagerly.

I could see that he assumed I had agreed to go, and I did not make any more objections. I stood up and said:

'Will you let down the ladder for me?'

He peered into my face and saw my purpose as clearly as if I had announced it.

'You're going to leave me,' he twittered. 'You're going to go down the ladder and back to the village and home to Borris in the morning!'

This was exactly the decision to which I had come. In the last moment it had become clear to me that the most sensible thing I could do would be to walk off quietly by the way that I had come, and let Uncle Martin get himself o t of his difficulties as best he could. But now he stood there in front of me, small and yellow and old, with the pleading eyes of an aged dog, and I could not find it in my heart to desert him. Something in the helpless way he looked at me appealed to my pride, too, and it was this more than anything that made me change my mind.

'No, no!' I said. 'You must trust me. You have told me nothing of what is happening, and still I am going to help you. I give you my promise that I will come back.'

That seemed to satisfy him. He gave his usual disagreeable smirk, which showed plainly his contempt for me.

'I'll trust you,' he said. 'You must go at once, then.'

He blew out the candle, and lifted aside the straw mat that covered the door. He did it so deftly that it was obvious he had spent a long time here. I followed him out on to the little platform, crawling around the mat as he did. The rain had stopped again and between the ragged clouds the sky was full of moonlight, so that the tree-tops showed up hard and black. Nearby a bird stirred sleepily. Uncle Martin was busily letting his ladder down to the ground. In a hissing whisper he said to me:

'Down with you, now. Throw up a stone when you come back, and I'll let the ladder down again for you.'

'Very well.'

I climbed down slowly, and heard him haul it up at once, as soon as I had set foot on the ground. I wondered how he managed the ladder when he was alone. Surely he did not leave it dangling for all the world to see. It occurred to me that he could tie a trailing ivy stem to the end of the ladder, and so pull it down when he returned to his tree. But how did he get the ladder up out of sight, after he had descended by it? I puzzled over this all the way along the little path, feeling my way in the intense darkness between the wet bushes. I had not arrived at the answer before I came out at the side of the house, into the clear moonlight.

I stood perfectly still, and listened. Now the wind seemed to thunder among the trees, and the branches creaked and moaned as if they must come crashing down. It would have been impossible to hear any sound above that din, and I gave up the effort after a moment and darted across to the shadowy wall of the house. I waited there, with every sense alert, until I was sure that there was no one following me. My heart was jumping about in a most uncomfortable way. The woods could have been full of watching eyes and I none the wiser. I wished I had not promised to return to my uncle, but I could not bear to leave him now, waiting hopefully for minute to minute for the signal to let down the ladder.

I edged along slowly to the corner of the house. A strand of some creeper trailed across my face and frightened me horribly. It took courage to put the tip of my nose around the corner, but at last I brought myself to do it. There was no one there. Only the stone lions sat on either side of the steps. I remembered that one of them had had his nose knocked off, and I took it as a warning of what might happen to my own. I had forgotten to to ask my uncle what had befallen the lion, but I knew he would not have answered. I was determined not to tell him a single word of my story until he would have answered this and all my other questions too. Then I would decide whether I wanted to have any more to do with him.

The thought of having my curiosity satisfied encouraged me to go on with my investigation. I slid along silently by the front wall of the house until I was under the drawing-room window. If the front door were shut, I thought, I could climb in here and pad around the house in my bare feet until I should have found the two men. It would be necessary to watch them for a moment before running back to the house in the tree with the news for Uncle Martin.

I was not very tall for my age, and I had to stretch upward on my toes to see the window. It was dark, and with the help of a strong ivy-stem that grew against the wall, I had soon climbed up and was sitting on the window-sill with my legs dangling. The little extra height gave me courage, I suppose, for I remember losing my fears all at once, and grinning to myself in the dark, and even whistling a few notes of a tune.

Then, with my hand on the window-frame to lift it up, I paused, and my inside seemed to curl up with terror. A soft light appeared within the room and a moving shadow, which was the door opening. In the space of a few seconds, the long-haired man walked swiftly into the room carrying a candle high and shading the flame with a gold-ringed hand. He came straight across to the window, to draw the curtains, I suppose, while I sat there on the sill and goggled foolishly. Then he saw me through the glass in the light of his candle. For a long moment we looked at each other, he with a kind of wonder, and myself, I am sure, with horror. Then very quietly he put down the candle.

I came to myself all at once. I was off that window and across the grass before the long-haired man could open his mouth to call out. Safe in the shadows I looked back once and saw the dim light still showing in the window. Then, above the noise of the wind, I heard the door burst open. I waited for no more, but made off like a fox in full chase down the avenue.

4   The Fahertys

I have never been able to go hunting since that wild race through the dark. Too well I know how it feels – the gasping breath, the stumbling feet, and above all the instinctive fear of the unknown pursuer, pounding relentlessly on one's track. I ran until my legs would no longer carry me. I was almost a mile away from the house, but in what direction I had not the faintest idea. I had come the whole length of the avenue on to the main road, and then I had plunged into a boreen on the opposite side. This boreen had forked. I had followed one branch of it at random, and now I was surely a good way up the mountain away from Cloghanmore House.

I stood on the grassy margin of the boreen and leaned against the stone wall. The clouds were gathering for more rain. It looked as if I might have to spend the night in the open, after all. I would not have minded this under the shelter of the Cloghanmore woods, but here it was dismally bleak. I thought of the house in the tree, and of my uncle waiting there for me, but if I had had to spend a month on the mountain-side I would not have returned to him now. I wondered if he had been trying to trap me, and had made an arrangement with his strange friends to send me to the house. Still, I was sure that if he had been playing a part he would have given himself away by giggling and smirking at the thought of deceiving me. However, all that was past now, and I hoped never to lay eyes on him nor on either of his houses again.

I began to walk along the boreen. Now that I was no longer

hot from running I could feel the bite of the wind. It whistled desolately through the holes in the loose stone walls and blew my wet clothes meanly against my body. I remember feeling that the world was a hard, cold place for a boy to travel alone.

My first sight of the warm lights from a cottage came like a comforting arm around my shoulders. Its little boreen led down to mine. The lamplight showed up a pattern of flowers on the curtains and while I stood there watching, a woman's shadow moved between. Without further thought I started up the boreen towards the house.

Before I came to the door I paused. I could not stagger into the house in my present state, covered with mud, my hair like a hedgehog's quills and my face streaked with sweat and dirt. I knew that my presence in the district would cause talk enough, and I did not want to tell my whole story unless I had to. If I were fairly clean and tidy, I could say that I was to my way to Galway and ask for a night's lodging. But first I must be sure that I did not look as if I had run a mile of mountain road.

I listened for the sound of a stream in which I could wash my face and hands, but if there was one, I did not hear it. Walking very softly, I went around to the back of the house, thinking I might find a bucket of water left outside. But the shadow of the house, with its projecting thatch, lay heavily there, so that I could see nothing. However, at the farthest gable I found a lean-to shed, and when I stood in the doorway I could feel dry ferns under my feet.

This would be a good place to rest, I thought, and to recover from my fright. I felt my way along the wall of the house, and presently my hand touched a furry ear. I followed it down to the head from which it grew, and felt it wag inquiringly under my hand.

'Good evening, Neddy,' I whispered softly. 'I'm going to shelter with you for a while.'

The donkey edged closer to me. I rubbed his hard forehead, and leaned against him to warm myself. I could imagine him

44

grinning away there in the dark, as donkeys do, and I stroked his long, stiff ears again. He was the first friendly being I had met since I had parted from Patrick Joyce this morning.

The donkey's supper of hay was piled in the corner behind him. I knew that it was hay by the feel of it only, for it was pitch-dark in the shed. He gave me leave to take a handful of it, and I rubbed myself down with it as if I were a donkey too. I sat down on the hay then, to rest my legs. I would almost have decided to spend the night here, but for the fear of being dis-covered asleep. There was no door, and if I did not happen to wake with the first light, anyone passing by could look in and see me. I could not trust myself to wake in time, for in spite of my long sleep in front of the fire in Cloghanmore House, I was beginning to yawn again.

At this point in my reflections I became aware that I was sitting on something hard. At first I thought of turnips, but the shape was wrong. I rummaged in the hay with my hand, and withdrew it slowly in astonishment. There was no mistaking the feel of what I had touched. Under the hay there was a little pile of long-barrelled guns.

I sat there for a long time, trying to think it all out. I could not help wondering whether the presence of the guns could have some connection with the hostility of the people of Clog-hanmore against my Uncle Martin. The fact that they were hidden under the hay, and that there were so many of them, showed that they were not merely sporting guns. It was hard to believe that there could be two feuds going on side by side in a quiet countryside like this. And yet, who would think of going out against Uncle Martin armed with guns? A man who took to the trees at the first sign of danger could surely be overcome by more peaceful methods.

The donkey nosed at me to see if I were still there, and I stroked him absently. Now I was quite certain that I could not spend the night in this shed, for anyone who discovered me would surely suspect that I had found the guns. It would be far better for me to keep to my original plan of pretending innocence and asking for a lodging for the night.

And it hardly seemed worth while moving on to another house, for I was as likely to meet trouble elsewhere as here. I whispered a word of farewell into the donkey's ear and went outside.

It was raining heavily again, and in the darkness I slipped into more than one puddle before reaching the front door of the cottage. It was opened within a few seconds of my knock.

A tall, middle-aged man stood there, looking at me. The light shone on the rain as it fell, so that it showed up in a beautiful pattern of little silver lines. I looked at the man without saying a word. He reached out and took me by the arm and led me into the house, shutting the door against the night with his other hand.

I found myself in a delightful kitchen, so bright and cheerful that it brought tears to my eyes. The walls were white-washed, and a big turf fire blazed on the hearth. On the red-painted mantel-shelf there was a clock in a wooden case, and photographs of relations of the family who had gone to America were ranged on either side of it. It was always easy to recognise these by the clothes. I knew that if in the course of conversation it came out that some of them were in Portland, Maine, where my Aunt Maggie was, there would be as strong a bond between us as if we had discovered that we were cousins. The dresser was filled with enough delph for a wedding, cups and saucers with fat red roses on them, and old, old plates showing pictures of farmers and dogs bringing home sheep. There were bowls for porridge, and mugs for tea and buttermilk, and a resplendent row of lustre jugs. The tall dash-churn stood beside the dresser, and a pat of newly-made butter was on the shelf beside it. A big oil-lamp hanging beside the fireplace lit up the room.

Standing at the table, ironing a shirt, was the woman whose shadow I had seen on the curtains. She was a remarkably handsome woman, slender and tall, and with smooth jet-black hair.

She wore the red petticoat and check apron that all my people wear, but around her shoulders she had an embroidered shawl of a kind that I had never seen before. Though she was not young, when she turned to put her iron to the fire to heat, she moved with the ease of a young girl. She looked at me humorously and said:

'Well, young man? Do you like my kitchen?'

I blushed and said:

'Yes, Ma'am.'

She looked at my muddy feet, and then at my wet coat and hair.

'Come over to the fire,' she said quietly. 'How long have you been out under the weather?' She turned to her husband. 'John, bring out Roddy's Sunday coat, like a good man. Come along now, young lad, and sit over on the hob.'

Her husband opened the door into the room behind the fire and came back in a moment with a heavy black jacket lined with fine satin, just the right size for me. I sat on the hob and took off my own jacket, but then the woman saw that my shirt was soaked too. She made me take it off, and gave me the newly ironed shirt off the table instead. Then she poured milk into a saucepan and put it to heat for me, and went to cut many slices of soda-bread to go with it.

The warmth of the fire and of my welcome put new life into me, and I felt a pleasant glow spread right through my being. Boys are always hungry, and in spite of the duck, Maria, I was able to account for a great deal of soda-bread and butter. The man of the house ate some with me, from politeness. It was not until I had finished that they began to question me.

'You're out late by yourself, young lad,' said the woman. 'Where were you going to sleep the night?'

'Would you let me stay here?' I asked. 'I could sit on the hob all night. It will be fine and warm, and I won't be in the way.'

'We'll do better than that for you,' she said. 'There's my son

47

Roddy has a bed big enough for three, and he won't grudge you a share of it.'

I said that they were very good, and thanked them for their hospitality. The man shrugged his shoulders and said:

'Nonsense. We like to see strangers now and then.'

Very delicately then, they began to question me about myself, where I had come from, where I was going, why I had come so far from the main road and many other questions whose answers gave me trouble. There were long pauses in the conversation, and they never seemed to press me too hard, but gradually I began to feel that they knew far more about me than I had told them, and that they knew, too, exactly where I had mixed truth and falsehood.

Presently the man took down a piece of wood from the mantelshelf, and began to whittle at it with a short-bladed knife which he had in his pocket. The chips flew into the hearth as he turned it in his hands. He told me that he was making a doll for a neighbour's child, and he showed me how he had jointed its arms and legs with pieces of wire so that they moved freely. When he had finished it, he said, his wife would make clothes for it. Then he showed me other things that he had made: a flour-bin carved with ears of corn, and a work-box with his wife's name, Anna, in tiny coloured shells on the lid. Lastly he showed me a perfect little model of a stagecoach, with steps for getting into it, and shafts, and a turntable, and upholstered seats inside. He had even put little lamps at the sides. I was completely enchanted with it, and I thought that he must be the happiest man in the world. He told me that he had an old picture of a stage-coach, which he had used to make his model.

Now that we had become so friendly, my fears were quieted and I thought I would try to find out more about the strange things that I had seen and heard since I had come to Cloghanmore. Casually I asked:

'Do you see many strangers in these parts?'

'Very few at this time of the year,' he said, bending his head again over the doll. 'In summertime people come now and then, but with the first autumn storm they go scuttling home again out of the cold. There's nothing for those people in Cloghanmore.'

'The trawlermen come sometimes, I suppose, and the foreign fisherman,' I said.

'Seldom enough,' he said, looking at me sharply. 'Did you see some of them to-day?'

I began to be sorry that I had spoken, but I could not draw back now. I said, as coolly as I was able:

'Yes, I saw two strange-looking men this evening. One was tall and the other short. But the queerest thing was that the tall one's hair grew down to his shoulders.'

'And where did you see these men?'

'Down on the shore. . . .'

Too late, I saw that I had given myself away. How could they even pretend to believe me now? I had said that I was on my way into Galway by the main road, and had lost my way. Whatever chance there was that I might have wandered up the mountains, I could not possibly have gone down to the shore by mistake as well. The man put his knife into his pocket, without a word, and replaced the wooden doll on the mantel. Then he said, very quietly:

'And what brought you down to the shore?'

I did not even try to make an excuse, but sat there staring at him. After a moment he said:

'Come now. I won't eat you. You are Jim O'Malley, aren't you?'

I nodded, but I could not bring myself to speak. He looked up at his wife for a moment, and then he said gravely:

'I'm very glad to know you, Jim. My name is John Faherty.'

He reached for my hand and shook it solemnly. I found my voice at last to croak:

'How do you know who I am?'

'It's not very hard at all,' he said, and leaned back in his chair to look at me. 'You had your breakfast with Patrick Joyce this morning, and you passed through Cloghanmore not long afterwards. You went straight out to the big house, but there was no one there, so you had a good sleep in front of the fire. You disappeared afterwards, and we lost track of you. But I'm thinking you must have seen that pair of queer hawks landing off the *Saint Brendan* and going up to the house.'

It may be imagined how astonished I was at this accurate recital of my day's activities. It was unpleasant to think of all the eyes that must have watched me on my way, while I had thought myself unnoticed. Even while I was asleep in the big chair in front of the kitchen fire, it seemed that someone had peered through the window at me. This thought I found especially horrid.

'I didn't see you myself,' John Faherty explained. 'I was busy with other things. You couldn't have met the foreign sailors anywhere except on the path from the shore to Cloghanmore House, for we know that they went there directly after leaving the boat.'

Suddenly I saw light.

'Your son is called Roddy,' I said softly.

'That's right,' said Mrs Faherty quickly.

'Yes, yes,' said her husband.

'Did you hide behind the wall and watch the long-haired man and his friend land? I heard you talking. Roddy said he would finish off the small one with his knife – '

Mrs Faherty gave a shriek, and leaped to her feet.

'John, John! What did you do to the foreign sailormen? Did you attack them, after all that I said? Where is Roddy now? Why hasn't he come back home?'

'Now, now, Anna! Don't be frightened. We didn't lay a finger on them. Did we, Jim?'

He looked at me with annoyance, and I must admit that I got no small pleasure from having the upper hand of him, for a change. I had the answer to my question, too. John and his son Roddy, whose coat and shirt I was wearing this moment, were the pair who had made my blood run cold earlier in the evening.

'No, Ma'am,' I said. 'They didn't touch them at all. They just watched them land and then they came away.'

She sat down with a long sign of relief. I used my advantage to ask:

'Why did Patrick Joyce bother to tell about me?'

'Because you said you were going to Cloghanmore House,' said John soberly, 'and anyone going there has to be watched.'

'But why?'

'Don't you know why?'

'I can't make out what is happening here,' I said. 'I never met so many mysteries in all my born days.'

'Yes, that may be true,' he said, nodding slowly. 'In her letter to your Uncle Martin, your mother did not seem to know what was going on either.'

I was about to protest against anyone suspecting either my-self or my mother of dishonesty when I remembered, just in time, the story I had told of being on my way to Galway on business for my father. This recollection also prevented me from showing offence at his knowledge of my mother's letter. It was clear that some of the local people had actually been in the house and had read the letter, perhaps even this very morning, before my arrival. No wonder that Fursey, the cat, had scarcely bothered to turn his head to look at me. He had probably seen so many strangers about the place that he no longer took any interest in them. What a story he could tell, if he were not so lazy!

'Where did you go after the foreign sailors landed?' John Faherty asked now, 'You did not go into the house with them.'

'No,' I said. 'I didn't like the look of them, any more than you did. I went into the woods.'

'Then you didn't meet your Uncle Martin at all.'

I made no answer to this. He sounded very disappointed and

it was obvious that he knew nothing of the house in the tree. Innocently I asked:

'Where is Uncle Martin now?'

'That's a question that every man in the barony of Cloghanmore would like to hear answered,' he said fervently. 'It's like looking for an eel in Galway Bay, so it is.'

'Maybe Jim knows where his uncle is,' said Mrs Faherty quietly.

'How could he know?' said her husband. 'Didn't he spend the day waiting for him in the house?'

'Why did you come out of the woods again, Jim?' she persisted.

'I came back to the house to see if there was any sign of the strangers,' I said. 'I thought I might be able to watch them, unknown, and to find out what is going on here.'

This was the exact truth. She nodded eagerly and asked:

'And what did you see?'

'I saw the long-haired man through the window, and he saw me. I ran for my life.'

'You did right,' she said. 'He probably thought you were one of us. Did he follow you?'

'I didn't wait to find out,' I said. 'Before the door was open, I was off.'

They nodded slowly, and an understanding look passed between them. I think it was this more than anything that exasperated me.

'What is all the mystery about?' I burst out. 'Which side is in the right? And why is this feud going on at all? You needn't think I'll side with Uncle Martin, if he is in the wrong. From what I've heard of him, I'd say he must have done some terrible injury to the people of Cloghanmore.'

'He did that,' said John Faherty. 'But blood is thicker than water, and I'd hardly expect his own nephew to condemn him.'

'I'm not sure that Uncle Martin's blood is much thicker than water,' I said drily.

They looked at me in silence for a moment, and then Mrs Faherty said:

'If you don't know the story already, it's time you were told, and if you do know one side of it, it will be a good thing for you to hear the other side.'

'It's too dark now to show him the place,' said John. 'It would be better to wait until morning.'

Mrs Faherty agreed, and I think I might have burst with rage and curiosity if the door had not opened just then and diverted my attention. The night wind blew a few straws across the kitchen floor and the little glimpse of rainy blackness outside increased the feeling of sheltered comfort within the house. Then the boy who had come in advanced silently towards the fire, never once taking his eyes off me.

'This is Jim O'Malley, Roddy,' said his mother. 'Don't stare at him.'

But he continued to do so. He was about my own age, I thought, or a little older. He was nearly as tall as his father, so that as I sat there on the hob I had the impression that he was towering over me in a threatening way. I may have been right, too, for his father suddenly spoke sharply:

'Roddy! You're making Jim feel uneasy. Come over and shake hands.'

He did as he was told, in a kind of malignant trance from which he only recovered when his father went on heartily:

'Jim, here, doesn't know a word about his uncle's tricks. He thinks he has rambled in among a lot of mad-men.'

Roddy spoke for the first time:

'That's what he must think, indeed, if he doesn't know the story. Does he know where Martin Walsh is now?'

'No,' said John Faherty. 'I'm telling you, he's as much at sea as we are ourselves, and worse.'

I said nothing. I had not by any means made up my mind to betray Uncle Martin as soon as I would have heard the story, for I feared that these people might injure him in their anger.

Whatever he had done, I did not want his blood spilt.

Roddy went across and sat down on the other hob while his mother prepared a meal for him. John Faherty took down the doll again, which I interpreted as a sign that there was peace between us. As he worked at it he said:

'We're going to tell Jim, here, the whole story in the morning. I'd tell him now, only we ought to show him the place first. After all, it's not that much of a secret. And if we catch up with Martin Walsh in time, it will all be in the newspapers anyway.'

'True for you,' said Roddy. 'But I'd rather catch Mr Martin Walsh before we start telling anyone about it.'

'We're going to tell him in the morning,' said his father firmly. After a pause he said: 'Did you see Scoot?'

'I did,' said Roddy. 'There was a crowd there, and he said they would be over for the boat at once.'

They said that they had had the *Saint Brendan* at the quay in the village, but that the foreign sailor-men had landed from a dinghy and slipped her out under the nose of their sentry.

Then they began to talk of other things, of people in Borris that they knew, and of the relations in America. These were not in Portland, but in Boston, though they agreed that Portland was a very good place too. John Faherty said he had known my mother well when she was young.

'She was the best-looking girl in these parts,' he said, 'and the best you ever saw to start up a dance or a song. A few the like of her would keep a whole townland happy.'

He said that he sometimes brought cattle to the fair in Borris, and I pressed him to come and visit my mother the next time. I told him that our house was the meeting-place for all the neighbours, and that my mother could not see a crowd together without ranging them in sets and half-sets, and getting music going for a dance.

'I'm too old for that now,' he said, with a grin at his wife. 'But I do like to be watching the young people.'

When Roddy had finished his supper we stood up to go to

bed. Mrs Faherty said that I was to share his bed, and he told me, shortly enough, that I was welcome. The clock on the mantel pointed to midnight.

Roddy lit a candle, and we went into the room behind the fire, leaving the older people to cover the fire with ashes and lock the door.

I had meant to question him about the doings of the day, and to get the whole story out of him while we lay in bed, but he hardly spoke to me at all, and I found it too difficult to begin. Watching him as he lay there staring at the ceiling with his dark eyes, I thought how much older than me he was in his ways. If I had had a secret like this, and another boy to share it with, I could not have stopped myself from telling it at the first opportunity. Indeed I would have been appealing to him to listen to me. Roddy was an unnatural boy, and no mistake.

Then why did I not tell him about Uncle Martin, hiding in a tree like a squirrel? Why did I not tell about the house in the tree, surely the most wonderful secret a boy ever had? With some regret, I realised that I was as close-mouthed in my own way as Roddy. This was the beginning of growing up, I supposed, and instead of making me feel melancholy the thought brought me nothing but satisfaction.

I climbed briskly into bed besides Roddy, and he blew out the candle. It was a chaff mattress, and it tickled unmercifully, but I did not feel it for long. I scarcely had time to stretch out at full length before falling fast asleep.

5 Uncle Martin's crime

When I awoke in the morning, Roddy's place beside me was empty. I lay there for a few minutes, marvelling at how deeply I had slept, and examining the room which I had but dimly seen in the candlelight last night. The big solid bed and the cupboards had obviously been made by John Faherty himself, for they were all carved with animals and birds and flowers. I thought they were the most beautiful things I had ever seen. The quilt was patchwork, not just stitched together anyhow, but finely embroidered at all the joins. John and his wife were surely a remarkable pair.

When I got out of bed I saw that my own clothes, quite dry and freshly pressed, were laid on a chair waiting for me. I put them on quickly and went into the kitchen.

'Just in time, Jim,' said Mrs Faherty from the hearth, where she was making tea.

Roddy came in with two frothing pails of milk as she spoke, and put them on the long bench over by the churn. Over his shoulder he bade me a short:

'Good morning.'

A moment later I heard John clattering with buckets outside, and then he came in too, and went across to wash his hands in the tin dish by the back door.

'It's a queer world,' he said heartily, 'where the pigs must get their breakfast first and the humans afterwards. How did you sleep, Jim?'

'Like the dead,' I said.

'Come along now, and eat like the living,' said Mrs Faherty, as she brought the teapot to the table.

She had a brown egg for each of us, and soda-bread and butter. I was amazed at their kindness to me, for surely to them I represented the enemy. But they showed no sign of enmity this morning, except that Roddy was still rather silent. He seemed to find it hardest to appear friendly, and I thought he had not quite made up his mind about my good intentions.

It was a wonderfully clear autumn day. Through the open door I could see comfortable-looking hens pecking at the ground in a leisurely, half-humorous way. The sunlight gilded them, so that they looked as if they might lay golden eggs at any moment. While I watched, one of them poked her head in and looked at us sideways, but she did not venture any further.

'She knows better than to try it,' said Mrs Faherty fiercely, with her hands on the sweeping-brush. 'One step more, Mrs Hen and I'll knock out your tail-feathers!'

The moment we had finished, John Faherty said:

'Will you bring around the horse and cart, Roddy, and I'll start telling Jim the beginning of the story.'

Without a word, Roddy stood up and went outside. His father looked after him thoughtfully, but made no comment. After a short pause he sighed and said:

'I'm sure I'm doing right. What do you say, Anna?'

'You must tell Jim,' she said. 'It's the only sensible thing to do now. After you have told him, you can make sure he stays here until the whole job is finished. Don't mind Roddy. He's at an age when there is only black and white, and if you're not for him, you must be against him.'

I said nothing at all, though I could have said many things about her bland suggestion that I be kept a prisoner. There was time enough to see about that later. I could see that John had not thought of this, for he glanced at her sharply and then, looking more satisfied, he began his story at last.

'First I must tell how I come to travel through France at all,' he said, 'and to see the thing that first opened my eyes.'

'It goes back a great many years, to the time when I used to go fishing with my father when I was a young lad. The fishing was quite good hereabouts, but sometimes we used to go a long way from home, if the weather was fair. I suppose they do the same in your part of the country?'

'They do,' I said. 'My father has been to Cornwall and Brittany, and he even went to Spain once. He said it was too hot for him.'

'I never got as far as Spain,' said John, 'though I have been invited many a time, by the trawlermen. But we often went to Brittany, and my father had lots of friends along the Granite Coast, as they call it. It's a terrifying coast to a Connemara man. For nearly a mile out into the sea, huge rocks are scattered, some of them sticking up out of the sea and others just covered with water at the high tide. At low tide the sea goes out a great distance and leaves them bare, and the local people have a name on every rock of them. It's well for them that they have. To see a small boat sailing round and about and in and out through the rocks would frighten the heart in you. My father thought he knew that coast well, but we sailed in there one blustery night, just falling dark, and didn't we strike one of those blessed rocks. It was called the Great Seal, and it was well named. Do you know the way a seal pulls himself up on to a rock, half out of the water, to take a look at the surrounding country? Well, this was like the biggest seal you ever saw. It was perfectly shaped, one big rock lying on the other, with part of it sticking forward like the head would be. There was even a bit of seaweed growing on the front of the head, for all the world like a seal's whiskers. I had plenty of time to study it, for the boat foundered and sank, and we were left clinging on to that seal's back, like the boyoes that used to be riding the big fish in the old stories.

'It was a good thing for us that it was not quite dark. We sat up there on the seal's shoulders, with the spray dashing over us, yelling murder, until we saw a boat putting out from the shore. The weather was not cold, and all that was worrying my father was that after this experience I would take fright of the sea, and never go sailing again. It didn't work that way with me at all. It was like the first time you fall off a horse. Thinking about it beforehand is much worse than the reality. I felt that I wasn't a man at all until after I had been shipwrecked, though I found out later that that is the height of foolishness.

'Well, we were brought ashore and feasted like kings, and in the morning we went out and salvaged the boat. She was a sad sight, with her sails in ribbons and her gear lost and a great cavern of a hole in her side. It was going to be a long job repairing her, and we had no money to do it with. Besides, we could not be away from home too long, for we were farmers as well as fisherman, like everyone else in these parts. But we need not have worried. As soon as the boat was ashore, and they had seen the extent of the damage to her, the people came together and decided to repair her for us.

'At first we said we would not let them, but they insisted on having their way. They said that this kind of thing had often been done for them in Ireland, and that they were only repaying former kindnesses. Of course we knew that this was true, but the Bretons are a comfortable people, and they could always do more for us than we could for them. However, we gave in at last and set out for home overland, because it was autumn and there were no boats going to Ireland at that time. They even gave us money for our passage home, and would not let us promise to pay it back. They were very good people.

'The following spring, when the good weather came again, they brought home our boat like new, only with red sails instead of black ones. But by the time the boat came home, an idea had begun to grow in my mind, which was the beginning of the changes that have come about in these parts.

'It was while we were travelling through France, in the Pas de Calais, that I saw how the people there had made good land out of swamps, and I was determined that when I got home we should do the same. I had only a few hours in which to study it as we travelled along, and the rest of the way home I could hardly think of anything else. I was planning how we could set to work at once, with no cost except our own labour, and within a few months drain the big valley that we are going to show you now.'

'You're making a very long story of it, John,' Mrs Faherty interrupted at this point.

'That can't be helped,' said John. 'He should know how it all started. The next thing is to show him what we did.'

At this moment, with a great clattering, Roddy drove the horse and cart to the door. He stood high in the cart, holding the reins, and called to us to come out.

'Come along, Jim,' said his father. 'I'll be telling you the rest of the story as we go along.'

We climbed into the cart and sat on the cross-board together, while Roddy still stood in front of us. Then he jerked the reins and the horse moved off. We waved to Mrs Faherty, who came to the door to watch us go.

John could not speak while the cart bumped and banged through the stony boreen, but when we got on to the smoother road outside and began to move westwards, he went on:

'The moment we got home I explained the whole plan to my father. He would not listen to me. He said the Connemara people had always been poor, and that if we could make a living at all between the fishing and the turf and the little bit of farming that we could do, we should be mighty thankful. I argued with him until my tongue was dry, and until I had used up every single word that I knew, but it was no good. He said young people were always full of these cracked notions, and that I'd better not say anything about it to the neighbours or they would think I had taken leave of my senses.

'You can imagine how hard it was to keep a dream like that bottled up inside me. There were times when I thought it

would kill me, and at last I tried to forget it. I did forget it for a while, when I got married and my father and I worked together on the land, and I had to hold my tongue for the sake of peace. He was a good, hard-working man, my father, but he had no vision.

'Then, eleven years ago, he died. I remember looking down at him at the wake, wishing him good-bye, and even with tears in my eyes thinking to myself: "Now I'll drain the big valley."

'I waited only a week. The big valley belonged to several of us, but we never did anything with it. There was no turf there, and it was too wet for sheep except in a very dry summer. My cousin, Scoot, who has the forge in Cloghanmore, and Spartóg and Michael Mór Nee – we all had a share in it, and a few more besides.'

'Why is he called "Scoot"?' I asked.

'Because if small boys come into the forge to watch him at work he shouts "Scoot!" at them,' said John with a twinkle in his eye. 'A very good reason. Well, I got Scoot and Spartóg together first and told them my plan, and that I had seen it work in France years before. They saw at once that we should try it, and they went to see Michael Mór Nee and the rest of them. The end of it was that on a certain early summer evening, when we had all the regular work done, we assembled in the big valley with spades and sleans, and began to dig the dykes.'

'I was there too,' said Roddy softly.

'So you were, with a small shovel of your own – a very small one. It was terrible work lifting the wet earth full of roots and heaving it up into banks. But we were used to doing this kind of thing, and we kept at it. It was only a few days before we saw the first signs that our plan was going to work. Water was seeping into the new dyke, and the banks were getting firm so that we could walk on them.

'You'll see in a moment what we did. We were never short of helpers, and when the people saw what we were at they came every evening to work at the digging. It was two years before we were able to begin to use the land, and every year since we have gone on with the work. Seeing my dream come true was the strangest and the most wonderful thing that ever happened to me.'

He fell silent, thinking about it. We were bowling along on the sandy road in the sunlight, while the young horse stretched his neck eagerly so that Roddy had to keep a firm hand on the reins. Down on my left the sea lay as smooth as a pan of milk. The tide was low, and the rocks were covered with the brilliant orange-coloured weed that grows so freely here. The sun warmed our backs as we sat in the cart. I turned and looked behind me in the direction of Cloghanmore village, and my eye fell on the woods about my uncle's house. With surprise I realised that this was the first thought I had given him this morning. He had been in the back of my mind all the time, I suppose, but now I suddenly saw a vision of him marooned in his tree, waiting for my return, and quite convinced by now that I had deceived him.

John Faherty looked so gently happy at this moment that I did not ask him where my uncle came into the story. No doubt I would hear soon enough. Just now I was enjoying the feeling of friendliness between us, and I did not want to spoil it by reminding them that Martin Walsh existed at all.

Our sandy road had begun to go downhill, and we were coming nearer to the sea. The main road from Cloghanmore had joined ours half a mile back, they said, and from now on ours was the only road to the west.

We did not come on the valley suddenly. Gradually it opened out on our right hand, as the hills moved back in a long curve that went around in a half-circle to the sea again. It was not so much a valley as a great plain, open at the side that faced the sea. With the misty autumn light it was hard to guess at the size of it, but it seemed to me to be about a mile and a half either way. The road ran along the seaside, and the cart continually crossed tiny bridges over the little canals that drained the land. These canals were about four feet wide, and were filled with black, boggy-looking water. Here and there light wooden bridges had been built over them so that one could go easily from one plot to another.

In between the canals there were smooth fields, some with stubble where a corn crop had been cut, others with potatoes still growing, and others again with turnips, mangels and sugar beet. I had never seen the like in my life, though I had heard that in the eastern and southern parts of Ireland there were vast fields with never a hill nor a hollow nor an outcropping rock from end to end of them. But that such a sight should be here in Connemara was unbelieveable.

I must have looked surprised enough to satisfy John Faherty, for he said in an offhand way that did not by any means conceal his pride:

'Of course we could not have grown these crops if the valley had not faced south. It gets the sun all day, and the mountains shelter it unless the wind is directly from the sea. That doesn't happen very often. Pull up the horse, there, Roddy,' he said 'and we'll take a trip around the canals.'

Roddy did this, and the horse went at once to the grassy edge of the road and began to graze, with the reins trailing. A few yards ahead of us a bridge spanned one of the canals, and a strange-looking boat was moored below. It was built high, for carrying crops and seaweed for manure, John said, and it was pointed at both ends because it could never be turned in the narrow canals. He said that there were several of these boats, and that he had seen them first on the little canals in France.

'Of course we made them all ourselves,' he added.

It was like a fairy-tale, stepping into the boat and moving slowly through the network of canals. Clouds of squawking sea-gulls rose up before us as we moved along. Roddy stood up in the bows and pushed against the banks with a long pole. The banks were built high, so that we had to stand too in order to see over the top. As we went, John showed me how the plan had developed, and how much work was still to be done.

'It has been worth all the trouble,' he said. 'The first year, we planted potatoes. We manured them with seaweed, as we always do. None of us will ever forget the crop we got. It was like digging gold. You never would have thought so many potatoes could grow on every stalk, nor such fine ones. The whole village came out to harvest them for us, and after that the few people who were still saying we were foolish got very quiet.'

Later they had experimented with other crops, and had bought suitable manures so that they were successful. John had got books of all kinds, and had learned how to handle the less familiar crops. They had planted trees, Austrian pine and Scotch fir, and larches for boatbuilding. He showed me the young trees growing bravely, not yet big enough for cutting. The owners of the valley had prospered.

'But it was not so much the bit we made out of this valley that pleased us,' he said. 'It was the way the people round about began to think that a few new ideas would be no harm – that was the best thing that came of it. That was why they listened when we began to talk about the lobster fishing.'

'I saw the men coming in with lobster-pots,' I said. 'Fine boats they have, too.'

'And why wouldn't they? There's hardly a fisherman in Cloghanmore that hasn't been able to build himself a new pookawn in the last few years. And high time, too. Most of them were only fit for matchwood, they were that old. You see, I happened to read somewhere that if you put a small lobster back into the sea and let him eat his fill, next year you'll catch the same lobster and he'll be twice the size – and worth twice the money. Lobsters don't travel far. The chances are that you'll catch him quite near where you put him back into the sea.

'This was a new idea to the people here. They thought that if you caught a lobster you should keep him because he was worth a couple of shillings anyway. A bird in the hand is worth two in the bush, they said. They thought that it would be going against God to put back the good lobster that He had sent you. That was at first. But then they remembered that I had been right about draining the valley. I brought the book down to the forge and read it for them, and we talked a long time about the habits of lobsters. Most of them knew that they grow a great deal between one year and the next, and that they don't wander far, and at last they agreed to try it.

'Then we had to make them swear that they wouldn't go after lobsters out of season. Once they agreed to that, the worst of the trouble was over. Some of them sneaked home with an odd small lobster, but mostly they stuck to the plan, and bit by bit we got all the backsliders to do the same.

'Well, to cut a long story short, it worked perfectly. The people began to make fortunes out of lobsters. We haven't any trouble selling them.'

At last I asked my question:

'Where does Uncle Martin come into all this?'

There was a short pause. In the silence I could hear the water ripple away from the bows of the boat. Suddenly Roddy lunged savagely at the bank with his pole, so that the boat rocked from side to side shooting up the narrow waterway.

'Steady, Roddy, or we'll be overboard' shouted his father. Then he went on slowly: 'Martin Walsh came in at the end. He has lived a sort of hermit's life for years since his sister went away. He'd go over to Cloghanmore of a Saturday for two loaves of bread and a little bit of bacon that wouldn't feed a sparrow. If there was no one in the shop he'd stay and have a few words with Paddy Conneeley, but the minute anyone would come in – even a child for a hen-egg's worth of bread-soda – he'd shut his mouth and march out without a word of good-bye. We all thought he was a shy sort of a man, but we were wrong. Mean, that's what he was. So mean that he couldn't give as much as a good word away.

'Well, the people began to make a bit of money, as I was saying, and the first thing that everyone did was to build a new boat. Then we got wood and made bits of furniture for the houses, and then we bought nice curtains and clothes for our wives and children. It was my cousin, Scoot Faherty, that had the next idea. He went in to Galway one day, and he heard them saying that there was great money to be made out of the *slat mara*.'

I knew this stuff well. It is a long, thick seaweed, like a heavy rope, and it grows abundantly all along our coast.

'Scoot asked a question or two,' John went on, 'and he learned that it would not cost much to start a factory for making the *slat mara* into powder, for making paper and wall-board and all kinds of things like that. He came home full of his idea, that we were all to pay in to a fund for starting the factory. The men were delighted with the idea. There would be work for everyone, drawing the weed, and in the factory too. We'd get a manager out from Galway. The whole world would hear about the marvellous things that were being done in Cloghanmore.

'Then for the first time we could not come to an agreement. It was about who was to hold the money. Paddy Conneeley refused to have it in the shop. That was the first place we thought of. He said he wouldn't be able to sleep at night for thinking of it, and that it might get mixed up with his own money. Most of us live in little houses far away from each other, and we didn't want it either, for fear any tramp walking the roads would break in and steal it. The schoolmaster was only a few months here, and we did not know him long enough to trust him. God help us! The man we trusted had lived long enough with us, that we ought to have known him!'

I began to get a horrid premonition of what was to come. Being very careful not to look at me, John Faherty went on:

'Martin Walsh travelled in to Galway every second Wednesday of his life. We went to him and asked him if he would take our money to the bank for us each time he went. He must have been delighted with us. Every time he came home he showed us a proper receipt for the money. There was nearly eight thousand pounds there in the wind-up. Then, five days ago, he drew out the whole lot, and disappeared. We haven't seen hair nor hide of him since then, nor a trace of the money – the savings of every man, woman and child in Cloghanmore for the last five years.'

6   A meeting in the village

My guess had been right. Very delicately, they avoided my eyes, and gave me time to think over the extraordinary story. For a while my thoughts were in such a confused state that I bumbled blindly from one question to another with no idea of how to disentangle them. At last I realised that my chief feeling was one of relief. Uncle Martin was not yet out of reach. Perhaps he could yet be forced to return what he had stolen. But I remembered the way in which Roddy had stabbed at the bank of the canal a few minutes ago, as if he had hoped to find Uncle Martin impaled on his pole when he withdrew it, and I saw that I would have to be very careful not to reveal that I knew where he was hiding.

'Did you trust Uncle Martin so much that you let him put the money into the bank under his own name?' I asked.

'No, no. We were not so simple,' said John. 'It was in the bank in the name of the people of Cloghanmore, but we never saw that the man that put it in could take it out just as easy by forging the names of the two of us that were in charge.'

So he was a forger, as well as a thief. I remembered his cunning little face, with its pointed nose and whiskery ears. If he were determined to have the money, it would be hard to outwit him now. It was clear that he had planned the whole thing long in advance, for it had surely taken time to build the house in the tree. I wondered if he had the money up there with him, like a jackdaw.

'We have seen him with those two pirates often,' said John.

'They used to come in to the quay at Cloghanmore, or to the slip below the big house, and walk over to visit him. I'm thinking it's a strange thing that they should arrive just now, if it isn't that he wrote to them to come and take him away. I'd swear he had promised them a share of the money in return for their help.'

'Where is Uncle Martin's horse and trap?' I asked.

John was on to this at once.

'How did you know he had a horse and trap?' he said, his face suddenly full of suspicion again.

'There was a stable with hay in the manger,' I said, 'and the marks of wheels on the coach-house floor.'

'True enough,' said John apologetically.

I saw that I had almost given myself away, and while I drew a quick, shuddering breath of relief I determined not to ask any more questions for a while.

'We took away the horse and trap this morning. Now they have no boat to get away in either,' said Roddy with satisfaction. 'The *Saint Brendan* is tied up to Cloghanmore quay, and God help whoever tries to lay a finger on her next time!'

There was a pause while they both watched me closely. It was easy to see what they wanted me to say, and after a moment I picked my words carefully:

'I'll help you in every way that I can, so long as Uncle Martin is not injured.'

'If we get back our rights, we'll be satisfied,' said John. 'We don't want revenge. It wouldn't be Christian.'

As Roddy poled the boat back to the place where we had left the horse and cart, I was fully occupied with wondering how I could help without betraying Uncle Martin's presence in the district. From what I knew of Uncle Martin, I guessed that if the people were to catch him and shake him hard enough, he would be glad to tell where the money was, to save his skin. He looked as if he would cringe and cry if he were cornered. But I did not want to see him cornered. It seemed that they had cut off his retreat, however, by taking his boat and his horse. If I could only get back to him now, I thought, I might be able to persuade him to give up the money, but I could not see how I was going to get away from the Fahertys. For all their friendliness, I was certain that they would keep a sharp eye on me. If I were to try to leave them now, they would be convinced that I had been sent to spy upon them.

At the bridge, the horse stopped pulling the grass and looked down into the boat with interest. Roddy jumped ashore and hauled the boat close to the bank so that his father and I could climb out. Then he tied it to one of the supports underneath the bridge.

Suddenly the horse lifted his head and cocked his ears, and looked eagerly down the road. A moment later we heard the even, rhythmic beat of hooves on the sandy road and presently a horse and rider came into view.

'It's Spartóg,' said Roddy the moment he saw him. 'I wonder what's after happening.'

The man sat his horse easily, with that little careless sideways tilt that sometimes shows an accustomed rider. I nearly laughed aloud when he came closer, and I could see the reason for his strange nickname. It was his hair. It was the colour of sun-dried mountain grass, a sort of sandy brown, and it grew in every direction in a rough, tangled mass. 'Spartóg' is the Irish word for the top grassy sod of a newly cut turf bank. Roddy saw me looking at Spartóg's hair, and an answering light came in his eyes. It was the first time that he had shown any real friendliness for me, and I felt a little glow of pleasure. With his air of independence and efficiency, he was the sort of boy whose company I always enjoyed, and for this reason his watchful attitude to me had hurt me deeply.

Spartóg pulled up his horse and gave me a look of quick suspicion. Before he had time to speak, John Faherty said:

'It's Jim O'Malley, Spartóg. He came along to Cloghanmore all innocent-like, expecting his Uncle Martin to put the newest

71

of food and the oldest of drink in front of him.'

Spartóg gave a short, sour laugh at the idea, so that I felt myself blushing for my uncle's reputation. Roddy noticed this and
said quickly:

'Jim did not know anything of Martin Walsh's tricks until
we told him.'

'Didn't he, now?' said Spartóg, and coughed apologetically.
'Then 'twas a sore disappointment to you, Jim.'

'It was more than that,' I said bitterly. 'It's a terrible thing
to have an uncle that's a forger and a robber, and that the
people's insides turn sour at the very thought of him.'

I was nearly crying with vexation by the end of this speech.
My pride was in the dust, and I would have given a great deal
to have been able to abandon the whole affair and to run home
for protection to my own people. I hoped that my feelings did
not show too clearly in my face, and perhaps they did not, for
Spartóg said kindly:

'Well, man, sure it's none of your fault. There aren't many
people in the world who could parade all their uncles and aunts
and cousins for inspection.'

I knew this was true enough. As I began to recall the oddities
of some of my neighbours' relations I felt a little better. Mean-
while John Faherty was saying:

'Well, Spartóg, what brings you here in such a hurry? What's
the news from the big house?'

Spartóg hesitated for a second, and I could see that he was
wondering whether he should exclude me from the conversation.
Then he seemed to decide that this was not necessary, for he
said:

'Things are stirring there. One of the foreigners, the little lad,
went down to the slip to look at the boat, and of course he
didn't find it. He ran like a redshank back to the house, and told
the big fellow, and they have barricaded themselves in now, as
if they were expecting a siege.'

'What have they done?'

'Closed the shutters and put the big wooden bar up to the front door. We heard it falling into the sockets. There isn't much else they can do. And there's another piece of news too.' He turned deliberately away from me. 'Martin Walsh was seen today.'

'When? Where? What was he doing? Who saw him? Speak up, man!'

With his shoulders thrust forward and his elbows crooked as if he would attack poor Spartóg and squeeze the information out of him, John Faherty took the complete attention of the other two and gave me time to cover up my amazement. Then I shut my mouth firmly and listened with all my ears.

'Hold on,' Spartóg protested. 'There's no fear I won't tell you all about it.' John held himself in with awful restraint. Spartóg went on: 'It was this morning, while Pats Rua was watching the house. He had been at it all night and he was a bit sleepy, he says. He hardly knew whether he was waking or sleeping when he saw Martin Walsh standing just at the edge of the wood, the way a fox would stand, watching, before coming out into the open.

'Martin Walsh didn't see Pats. He stood there and cocked an ear, and then he trotted across the grass and into the big yard. The next thing Pats heard was the back door banging shut, and he knew that Martin had gone into the house.

'Pats didn't know what to do. He says he could have captured Martin if he had been quicker, but he got such a surprise that he let the chance go. He never took his eyes off the house until my Ned came along to take over from him, and there wasn't a stir out of the house since except the one time that the little lad went down to look for the boat. We were thinking that maybe Martin is inside still, and that they would have made a run for it if the boat had been there.'

'And Martin Walsh didn't leave the house since?' John Faherty insisted.

'We don't know,' said Spartóg helplessly. 'He could have

slipped away again unknown to them, maybe. But where would he go? Pats said he looked a bit battered, like a man that had been on a journey. He'd hardly go away again immediately if he had just come a long distance to meet the foreigners.'

'True for you. Did anyone see him going through the village?'

'No one. You'd think he dropped from the sky.'

I knew that this was just what he had done. No doubt he looked a bit battered, as Spartóg had said, because he had been sleeping in his clothes in the tree.

'So now it seems that he's hiding in the house,' said John slowly, 'and even if we broke in there we mightn't find him. There was always talk of a priest's room in Cloghanmore House,' he said to me, 'a secret room in the thickness of a wall maybe, where a priest used to stay in hiding for a while in the bad old times. There may be no truth in that, though, for people do be always making up yarns about old houses. Still, it's a queer thing if he stayed inside, where we'd only have to go and pick him out.'

I guessed that Uncle Martin had slipped away again, back to the tree, as soon as he had heard that the boat was gone. He would have been too careful of his skin to have risked staying in the house, even if there had been a dozen secret rooms there, I thought.

'So there has been no sign of life since?' said John.

'Only that the big man with the long hair was up at the top windows looking out to sea. Pats and Ned thought they might be expecting a boat to take them away.'

'And was there any sign of a boat?'

'The steamer on its way to the Aran Islands, and a pookawn or two from Casla way. And Mattie Folan's gleoteog, but we know he was going to Spiddal to christen his sister's new baby.'

I thought privately that there was not much these people did not know. It said a great deal for Uncle Martin's cunning that he had managed to evade them for so long.

'So now it looks as if they are expecting a siege,' said John slowly. 'Well, perhaps we won't disappoint them.'

'They won't stand a very long siege on the amount of food in that house,' I said.

'Perhaps they'll eat each other,' said Roddy. 'That would save us a lot of bother.'

'We must keep a look-out for a boat,' said John. 'They're surely expecting one. The *Saint Brendan* wouldn't have brought them very far, even if they had her.'

'Ned is watching the house, and some of the other lads are watching the sea, so there's time for a conference below in the shop before we start anything new,' said Spartóg.

'Are the men there now ?' asked John.

'They are, so. I came out looking for yourself and Roddy, and Anna told me you were above in the valley.' He turned a quiz-zical friendly eye on me, as if he had had time to think of me and had decided in my favour. 'She didn't say a word about young Jim, here.'

I had had some small hope that I might be left to look after myself while the men consulted together in the village. But it never occurred to them not to take me with them. Roddy and his father and I got into the cart, and this time John took the reins. Spartóg, who had not got off his horse at all, led the way at an easy trot. Our horse did his best to imitate the other, in spite of the heavy cart with its three passengers. The two sets of pounding hooves, the clattering axle and the grinding of the metal-rimmed wheels on the sand, all made so much noise that there could be no conversation. When the road forked we took the right-hand turning that went along by the sea. The sun was high overhead now, for it was after midday. Our trip around the canals had taken a good piece of the morning. Away out on the horizon I could see the deep blue curve of the nearest Aran Is-land, and the plodding black shape of the little steamer working its way out towards it. There was no sign of any other boat, not so much as a currach. I wondered why the men did not place some of their watchers in boats off the shore, but of course I felt no temptation to help them to improve their plans to catch my miserable uncle.

Passing the Cloghanmore woods, they kept their eyes fixed on the hazy trees as if they must surely read their secret. While we watched, two birds flew up, suddenly squawking, about where I knew Uncle Martin's nest to be. I held my breath until they settled again. No one said anything. Where the road skirted the estate we could no longer see the tree-tops, and my companions might peer as much as they pleased, for there was nothing to be seen except thick underbrush and withering ferns. The main gates looked desolate, with rust thick all over them. As soon as we had passed them, no one turned his head to look back, for now we could see the roofs of Cloghanmore village and the masts of the hookers tied up to the quay in front of us.

Presently we were pulling up before Paddy Conneeley's shop. Spartóg slipped off his horse in one quick movement and went inside. John Faherty made a great business of tying his own horse to a ring in the wall, shouting to the obedient and bewildered animal as if he were taming an elephant. But for all that he could not cover up what was happening inside the shop. As clearly as if I had been present, I could hear how a low hum of conversation had stopped when Spartóg went in, and then how his voice came softly but excitedly as he told the listeners that I was outside and would be coming in a moment to be looked over. I could not hear his words, of course, but I was in no doubt about what he was saying. Neither was John Faherty, for he gave me a somewhat rueful glance and then, without a word, led the way into the shop.

I was struck speechless the moment I stepped in through the doorway. It was a big shop, and well stocked with every kind of thing that could be used in a house, or a farm, or a fishing boat. There were sides of bacon and loaves of bread, flour-bins and tea-bins and sugar-bins. There were four big wooden barrels of porter on stands behind the counter. There were bottles of ink and packets of paper and envelopes for writing to America with. There were ribbons and aprons and tweed caps and stiff white collars. There were calf muzzles made of sally rods and leather winkers and straddles. There were fishing-nets and hooks big enough to catch a shark with, and beautiful big yellow coils of rope. It was a wonderful shop. But though my eyes travelled all around to see these things, they had to return unwillingly at last to meet those of the group of men who were standing at the counter, watching me.

I do not know what they had expected to see – a giant with eight legs and two heads, perhaps, and a club big enough to crush the whole seven of them at one blow. Their faces were full of grim purpose. Their hands were clenched with anger, and every man of them looked ready to spring forward at a word and attack me. But after a moment their expression softened. Though I represented their enemy, I was not nearly fierce enough for the part. One by one they relaxed, and presently a big, slow-spoken man in the middle of the group said humorously:

'Sure, there's hardly a bit of him there. Tell me, young boy, does your mother know you're out?'

There was a general laugh at this, the traditional question to a boy who is pretending to be a man before his time. I felt myself go hot with annoyance, but I made no answer. Each man had a big glass of black porter on the counter beside him, and now by common consent they all turned around and took a hearty drink. I availed myself of the opportunity to slip in behind John Faherty, who had taken his place at the end of the long counter. Roddy came with me, quite silently, with his eye on the men. Without waiting to be asked, the quiet-looking man behind the counter had milked a pint of porter out of one of the barrels and placed it in front of John, who lifted it now and took a very small taste of it before he said:

'Jim has promised to help us to catch up with Martin Walsh. As I was saying to Spartóg, here, he knew nothing of this until I told him. But he doesn't want his uncle to be hurt, and that's

77

a thing any of us would understand.'

All the men murmured:

'Of course. To be sure. No one wants to hurt him.'

And one added:

''Twould be nothing but a waste of time – like beating an old goat.'

There was a short, sour laugh at this, and then silence. At last the man behind the counter, whom I guessed to be Paddy Conneeley, said:

'And what can Jim do to help us?'

'Nothing, until we catch Martin Walsh,' said John. 'Then he could try and talk sense to him, and get him to give back what he stole.'

'A fat chance,' growled one of the men.

At that moment the door darkened. I turned to look, and saw that it was completely filled with the figure of a huge woman in a brown flowered shawl. She had a fat, contented face and grey hair, and she looked even bigger and rounder than she was because she had a large basket under her shawl. She puffed her way over to the counter, twitched aside the shawl and heaved the basket up, nearly knocking the nearest glass of porter.

'Now, Máire! Easy on, there!' said its owner, wrapping a protective hand around his glass.

'Wisha, Scoot, agrá, is it yourself that's in it, this hour of the day?' she said good humouredly. 'And why aren't you below in the forge about your business?'

I looked at Scoot with particular interest, because I had heard his name so often. He was not tall, but his shoulders were broad and heavy. He looked like a man with a temper, and I could well believe that he would have no patience with sightseers at the forge.

'It's Máire Spartóg,' Roddy whispered in my ear. 'Spartóg's wife.'

Máire was looking down the line of men, and now she gave a little hoot.

'And there you are, Spartóg, and I looking for you to tackle the ass for me. I couldn't catch him at all, the old divil, and I had to walk all the ways down with the chickens and the butter and all in the basket, and here you are now, Paddy, you can start taking them out now, and mind you don't break the eggs, there's a score of fresh eggs down under everything else, well I shouldn't say a score for that robber of a dog whipped one on me and I just putting them into the basket, so that's only nineteen. Oh!' she stopped suddenly and clapped a hand over her mouth. 'Maybe he took two, without I knowing! Lift out them cocks quick, Paddy, till I count them.'

While her head was buried in her basket, Paddy jerked his thumb in the direction of the room behind the shop. Roddy was nearest to the door, and he opened it for the men to file silently through, each carrying his glass and walking as if there were a dozen cross babies asleep in the corner. Paddy stayed behind, to keep Máire in talk, I suppose, and to attend to any other customers that might come in. I was the last to move, and when we were all inside Roddy shut the door and stood with his back against it. From the shop we could hear Máire's voice chattering away again, but fortunately we could not hear what she was saying.

Spartóg's expression was a mixture of sheepishness and truculence. No one said a word about his wife and gradually he relaxed. Scoot looked around the room and said:

'Well, boys, we'll be quieter in here, so we'll get down to business.'

We were in a little bare parlour that was probably rarely used, for there was a chill in the air of it. It had bright yellow wallpaper, the colour of a daffodil, with stout, hearty red roses scattered over it. I thought it was beautiful. There were a great many pictures on the walls, of cats and dogs and sheep and cows in country scenes very unlike ours. Over the mantel, in the place of honour, there was a framed certificate of some sort, but it was impossible to read what it was about for the print had

79

faded completely, as if it had never been except for the words: 'This is to certify', in grey twirling letters.

There were only four chairs. These were taken by John Faherty and Scoot and Spartóg, and the big man who had spoken to me first, and who now turned out to be Michael Mór Nee. The five other men stood about the little room, seeming to crowd it beyond endurance. Suddenly the air was full of menace, and the hard look was back on the dark faces around me.

'The time has come for action,' John began. 'We know that Martin Walsh and his friends are in the house. This is what we have been waiting for.' He looked around the group. 'Is there anyone here who feels that he can afford to let that mean, sneaking scoundrel away with the property of the people of Cloghanmore?' No one said anything. 'Very well. You know the plan. We talked it over often enough, and now the time has come to use it. We were to wait until we had him in the house, you remember. . . .'

Suddenly his eye lit on me, and he stopped. I stared back at him, with my mouth open, not knowing what was to come next. Then, in a completely changed tone, John turned to Roddy, and said:

'Your mother will be expecting us home, Roddy. Let you and Jim go back now and tell her she won't see us until evening.'

Without a word, Roddy opened the door and held it for me to pass out into the shop. Máire Spartóg was telling Paddy about the fox that had scattered her geese, and how she was going to circumvent him. She stopped in the middle of a word to watch us go out of the door, but before she had time to draw breath for her next sentence, we were outside untying the horse. A moment later we were plunging off up the street, in the way that we had come.

7 Back to Cloghanmore House

Outside the village the horse slowed down to a walk, and it was only then that we sat down on the cross-board. Abruptly I said:

'Do you know the plan they were going to talk about?'

'I do, that,' said Roddy grimly. I thought he was going to say no more when suddenly he burst out: 'And a mean, horrible plan it is, to my mind! That's what I told them, too. It's one thing to beat a man in a fair fight, but to burn down the house around him – that's like something Martin Walsh would do himself!'

I let the last remark pass, while I thought over the rest of what he had said. So they were planning to burn down the house. I had heard John talk about keeping on the right side of the law, and I wondered what the law would have to say to this idea. When Roddy and John had watched the strangers land it was Roddy who had been the bloodthirsty one, and his father who had tried to restrain him. I reminded Roddy of this conversation now.

'Your father sounded very peaceable to me then,' I said.

'It was only that he didn't want me to be the cause of killing anyone,' said Roddy. 'I was very cross that evening, and I suppose it was a good thing there was someone there to make me go easy. The men don't want to kill Martin Walsh at all, only to smoke him out into the open. But 'twould be a fright to the world to burn down a fine place like Cloghanmore House. Think of all the beautiful furniture and curtains and everything....'

I burst out laughing. Roddy looked at me in bewilderment.

'Have you ever been inside the house?' I asked.

'No,' said Roddy, 'but I've often heard tell of it.'

I described to him the part of the house that I had examined, and the battered furniture and moth-eaten curtains.

'Your own house is furnished in far better style,' I finished.

Roddy was truly astonished. All his life, he said, he had heard that Cloghanmore House was one of the finest in the country.

'Perhaps it was, at one time,' I said, remembering the curtains that one could see even now had once been splendid.

Then I began to fear that I might have done away with the only reason for not burning the house. Though the house itself would be no great loss, my soul turned sick at the thought of the two foreign men and possibly Uncle Martin being trapped inside. It was very well to say they would be smoked out, but who could say they would reach safety in time? And I remembered now the little pile of shotguns under the hay in the lean-to shed at Faherty's house. Perhaps if they ran out into the open to escape the fire, they would be shot down by the angry watchers. All at once I made my decision.

'Pull in to the side of the road, Roddy,' I said. 'I have something to tell you.'

Roddy did so, and as we sat there in the sun while the horse cropped the grass, I told him about the house in the tree. His eyes lit up with excitement as I described it.

'I'm sure my uncle is there now,' I said. 'He would never have stayed in the big house, for above all else he does not want the people to know that he is still in this district. It was bad luck for him that he was seen this morning. He has been going up and down every day for the last fortnight.'

Now at last I came to the idea that I had been turning over in my mind, but whose fulfilment depended altogether on Roddy's help.

'If we could get Uncle Martin and his friends away to another place, that they couldn't escape from, we could force them to give us the money and leave the country altogether. Then we could hand the money over to your father and everything would be settled.'

'What's wrong with telling my father about the house in the tree?' Roddy asked.

My heart sank. I answered very carefully:

'That would be just as bad as if they found him in the house. If we show Uncle Martin that we have the upper hand of him, there is some chance that he will tell us where he has hidden the money. But if he falls into the hands of the Cloghanmore men first, there's no knowing what might happen to him, and we might never hear where the money is.'

'There's sense in that,' said Roddy, 'and I know the very place to put them.'

'Where?'

'Inishgower.'

'Where's that?'

'It's a little, small island where we bring sheep for grazing. It belongs to my father and Scoot, but Scoot never goes there because he doesn't have sheep.'

An island was just what we wanted, of course. I said so, cautiously, for I did not want to press Roddy too hard. I need not have worried. He was fascinated with the idea by now, not only of saving Uncle Martin and his friends from the horrible hazard before them, but also of being himself the person to find the missing money and return it to its owners.

There was no time to be lost, though the men would probably not attack until nightfall, Roddy said. He shook up the horse and we drove along until we reached the little side road where I had met the goat on my first day. Now we had to dispose of the horse and his cart. We thought it would be cruel to leave him standing in the lane until our return, so we unharnessed him and turned him into a field by the roadside. We got the cart into the same field and pushed it well in under the shelter of the wall, so that a casual passer-by would not see it. Then we started off on foot down the little road to the sea.

I let Roddy lead the way this time. He knew every stone and every blade of grass, as I could see, and within a few minutes we reached the wall that skirted the wood. He told me that the boys in the neighbourhood kept away from the wood, for fear of Martin Walsh, though they would have dearly loved to play among the trees. It seemed that Martin had a reputation for being able to turn boys into rats. I had no doubt that if the wood had been a common playground for boys, they would have found the house in the tree long ago.

We got over the wall at the same place as I had done, and I was surprised at how clearly I remembered the way that I had gone. With painful caution we worked along, until at last we were at the edge of the clearing. Now, in daylight, I thought it would be easy enough to see the house. But beyond a sort of thickness in the branches, it was not visible even now. Perhaps when the tree would be bare, it would be different, but there was still a heavy covering of yellowing leaves. Silently I pointed it out to Roddy. He nodded, and then we went creeping across the grass until we were under the tree. Our bare feet made no sound, except once when I stepped on a twig which cracked softly.

Looking upwards, I saw a mere thread of ivy hanging, ending at the level of the top of my head. I pulled it gently, and down came the end of the rope ladder, so silently that I guessed its pulley was kept very well oiled. Roddy gave a tiny squeak of surprise before he could prevent himself. We listened, but no sound came from above. I pulled the ladder down as far as it would come, and then I began to climb up. Roddy waited until I was at the top before setting foot on the ladder, and in another minute he was at my side on the little platform. Though I thought I must have burst with the desire to turn my head towards the little house, we hauled up the ladder first and left it lying loosely at the edge of the platform. Then we crossed to where the straw mat covered the entrance to the house.

I lifted the mat outwards, and fixed it with a twig into the roof, so that it should not fall to again. Then I went down on my hands and knees and crawled through the doorway without a sound. I could feel Roddy on my heels, as silent as a shadow. Once inside, we moved away from the doorway, so as to let in the light. Roddy's eyes travelled in wondering delight all around the house, but mine had gone straight to the heap of bedclothes in the far corner. I clutched Roddy's arm. He followed my pointing finger, and we stood as still as mice when the cat's eye is on them. For a full minute we did not move.

Uncle Martin was lying there, curled up on the bedding like an old, old rat. He was fast asleep, with his wrinkled head between brown wrinkled paws. His eyelids were like blinds on the windows of a house of thieves. Every moment I expected them to spring up showing us clearly to his villainous beady eyes. But he did not stir, and I might have thought he was dead if he had not cleared his throat with a little querulous chirp, in his sleep.

That little sound sent us flying in fright out of the door, like two ghosts. There I looked back, and saw that he had not stirred. I let the mat drop back into place. Then I slid the ladder over the edge and we scurried to the ground. Even in our hurry, I did not neglect to haul the ladder up out of sight again, by the trailing ivy.

Back in the woods we held a conference. Roddy said that our best plan was to get the two foreigners away first, if we could, and then to tackle Uncle Martin alone.

'If he doesn't wake up and sneak off on us,' he finished.

'There's not much fear of that, by the looks of him,' I said. 'I'd swear he sat up all night waiting for me to come back, and that's why he's dead beat now.'

I felt somewhat guilty now at the thought of the good night's sleep that I had enjoyed in Roddy's bed, while Uncle Martin had sat peering into the darkness and listening to every rustling leaf, in the hope that it signalled my return. Roddy wasted no sympathy on him.

'A seasoned blackguard like that doesn't mind losing a few hours' sleep,' he said sourly.

But I had felt a surge of sympathy for the old rascal as he lay asleep. I was almost sorry now that we had stopped at the tree at all.

Roddy was quite undisturbed by any such notions, of course, and I was mighty glad that he assumed that I was equally hard-hearted. The truth was that he was the sort of person who always looked forward to the next task to be done, and who never wasted time on worrying about past mistakes or speculations. He was of a more practical turn of mind than I was, and now he took the part of leader quite naturally. For my part, he was quite welcome to it.

Even if we had been strong enough to overcome the two men by force and carry them off to the island, because of the daylight we judged that it would be unwise to try it. We had plenty of reason for not wanting to engage in battle. Though one of the men was very small, the other one more than made up for this in size. And both of them looked as if they would be quick with a knife. At this thought my peace-loving heart nearly failed me. Roddy seemed to be licking his lips at the thought of fighting them, but after we had talked it over for a minute or two, he agreed that we would have to use persuasion instead of force. He thought they would not be so hard to win over.

'They know now that the *Saint Brendan* is gone,' he said. 'They may have seen that the men are watching the house. We'll maybe find them very willing to come away with us to a safe place. You have a confiding way with you, Jim, that would make anyone believe what you tell them. You must talk them around slowly –'

'But you'll be there too!' I said. 'You don't think I'm going to tackle the pair of them single-handed?'

'Haven't you two hands?' Roddy retorted. 'And sure, I must go back to Cloghanmore and get a boat to take them to the island. I'll have to get the *Saint Brendan*, however I manage it.

If we have her, they'll believe that Martin Walsh sent us for them.'

I was too proud to let him see that I was afraid. Presently we were creeping through the wood again, on our way to Cloghanmore House. We followed the little path from the clearing, and at the edge of the wood we separated. Roddy went towards the front of the house where he was to have a word with Pats Rua. The idea was that he would divert attention from the house while I slipped across and got into the farmyard without being seen, and this I did. The soles of my feet seemed hardly to touch the ground as I fled across the few yards of open ground. Then I was at the back door, trying the handle. It was locked, of course. I did not want to make a noise, or I might have tried hammering on the panels.

The hen-house was built at right-angles to the house, and its pointed roof would bring me within reach of an upstairs window. I climbed on the wire-netted door and swung myself upwards to the rain-water gutter that ran at the roof's edge. The hens inside the house shrieked in horror at my audacity, but I was up on the roof and creeping like a snail up the sloping slates before they knew what was happening. Once up on the stone coping I sat with a leg dangling on either side and wished my head would stop swimming. Strange spots of various colours danced before my eyes. My neck felt stiff, and it was an effort to lift my eyes to the house, to discover which window would be the nearest and the easiest for my entry. I was convinced now, beyond any doubt, that it was mad to be trying what we had planned. I had never been able to influence anyone, so far as I knew, to follow my wishes, and yet here I was starting off to try to persuade two suspicious foreigners to believe in me as their rescuer.

Suddenly, all such logical thoughts drained out of me and ran away like sea-water in sand. Standing at the tall stairs' window, looking out on the hen-house roof, was the big man with the long hair. I felt myself slip sideways, and I grasped at the coping with both hands and righted myself. He did not move, nor did his expression change. At first I thought that he had not seen me. Then I saw that his eyes were fixed on mine unflinchingly. As for me, I must have been the picture of terror and astonishment. To be sure, I had intended to seek out the men in the house, but I think I must have expected them to be cowering fearfully in some corner, where they would have welcomed anyone who brought them a hope of rescue. Certainly I had never imagined that I would find them as collected as this cold-eyed stranger who even through the thickness of the glass had the power to turn me to stone.

He leaned forward without hurry and raised the window with both hands. In a deep voice, pitched low, but not in a whisper, he said:

'Come in, my friend. You seem to have a fancy for looking through windows.'

After all, I had come to help him, my brain chattered feverishly to itself, while he held the window contemptuously still. I edged along the roof towards him, with a sheepish, ingratiating smile which I blushed to think of afterwards. I swung one leg over the sill, and put my head and shoulders after it through the window. Then, all at once, his hand gripped the back of my neck like a lobster-claw, and he dragged the rest of me through, and held me so high that I had to stand on my toes. Through the coloured glass of the window, the sunlight lay in dusty bars of blue and red on the bare floor. I can still see the shape of them. Then, from above my head came his voice, unperturbed:

'Now we will go downstairs, and find out why you have come.'

He pushed me before him in a way that I found most humiliating, and painful too, for he never relaxed his grip on the back of my neck. He took long steps, so that I had to run to keep before him. Altogether I was in a sorry state by the time we had gone down the stairs and into the kitchen. It was a mighty poor beginning to our plan of capturing the two men and abducting them to Inishgower.

In the kitchen he released his hold of me with a little contemptuous push. I stood in the middle of the floor, like a frightened bullock at a fair, while the big man went across and sat comfortably by the fire in the grandmother's chair. With his thumbs in his waistband he lay back and stared at me, and I could not discover from his expression what thoughts were in his mind. There was complete silence in the room. I looked up at the ceiling and saw the spiders all gathered in one corner, laughing at me. I knew that I should not feel like a prisoner, for had I not set out to get into the house and talk with the big man? His dark eyes were as inscrutable as bog-holes, and I could get no lead from them as to how I should open the conversation.

He was a strange sight. He was dressed in a black velvet jacket and wide blue cotton trousers. He wore a pair of soft black leather boots tooled in gold, and when he hitched up the knees of his trousers to sit down I saw black socks embroidered with red flowers. Around his neck there was a wide red silk cravat, and a huge gold medallion, with a head engraved on it, dangled below it on a gold chain. All this, with his long black hair growing down to his shoulders, made him such an oddity that it was no wonder I did not find him easy company.

A last it was he who broke the silence, in the same deep resonant voice:

'Well, boy. What brings you here?'

'Uncle Martin gave me a message for you,' I stammered.

He raised his eyebrows.

'Uncle Martin? I know who you are now. He is a strange man. Did he send you here?'

I nodded. Uncle Martin had sent me, last night. The big man jerked his head towards the kitchen table, where my mother's letter lay spread out, and said sardonically:

'You are his nephew, Jim, sent by your good mother to learn the ways of the world from your Uncle Martin.'

I had to bite my tongue to prevent myself from saying what I thought of Uncle Martin's ways. All at once I thought I saw how to manage this man. His florid clothes, and particularly the gold medallion, were surely the signs of an arrogant, overbearing personality. Then my best plan was to play the innocent, and lull his suspicions by pandering to his pride. I said waveringly:

'Yes, I am Jim O'Malley. I only came yesterday. I don't know what is happening here at all, but my uncle says that everything is all right and proper, and that I should just do as he says.'

'Good boy,' said the big man impatiently. He had no interest in the scruples of my conscience. 'Give me the message from your uncle now.'

'But I must be sure I am giving it to the right person,' I said. 'What is your name, sir, if you please?'

He stood up, drawing himself to his full height.

'I am called Pietro,' he said, as if the name should have meant something to me. It was almost as if he had added: 'I am such an important person that I need only one name.'

'And your friend?' I asked innocently.

'He is called Miguel,' said the big man carelessly. 'He has another name, but I have never troubled to find out what it is. He is a person of no account, except that he is my servant.'

'Where is he now?'

I could see that he resented my questioning him, but he began to answer all the same:

'He is up at the top of the house, watching. . . .' He stopped, and a threatening note came into his voice. 'You do not ask any more questions. If you have a message, give it. If you have not. . . .'

Suddenly, he had a knife at my throat. The slow sunlight that came through the window caught the blade for a second so that it flashed like lightning. All at once, the unreal air had gone out of the interview. I could see now that I had been deceived by the fancy dress that this man wore into thinking, almost, that he was only playing at villainy. Now I realised that a man who actually goes to the trouble of dressing for the part of a pirate, and whose arrogance leads him to boast of his importance to a poor country boy, is a sad rogue indeed, and surely, as we say, past praying for. A cold sweat of bodily fear broke out on me, as if I had been trapped in a shed with an angry bull. I felt my fingers twitch and clutch each other, and I pushed my hands into my pockets to keep them still. Instantly he was upon me dragging them out again. The ridiculousness of his fearing anything from me helped me to regain possession of myself, and I said:

'I haven't got a knife. If I had same, there isn't much I could do to a fellow your size.'

He was preening himself again, ludicrously, but I would not for the world have laughed at him. For that crime, I guessed, he would have laid me out, dead, on the floor. Now that my voice was steadier, I was able to go on:

'I have a message from Uncle Martin. He says that you can't stay here any longer, because there's people watching you. Why would people be watching you, sir, if you're not doing any harm?'

'No questions, please,' he said sharply. 'What else did he say?'

'He said you're to come away in the boat with me,' said I hurriedly, 'and I'll bring you to a safe place.'

'What boat?'

'Uncle Martin's boat, the *Saint Brendan*, of course.'

'Ah, so it was he who had the boat taken away.' He nodded slowly, as if he were linking together a whole series of events. I did not explain any further. 'Is the boat at the quay now?'

'It will be there soon,' I said. 'We must wait for an hour or more, till it can be brought around to the quay. You can get ready now –'

'I haven't said that I am going with you,' he said.

For a while I feared that I had spoiled everything by my eagerness. He sat down again and looked at me broodingly, while I stood still in the middle of the room, afraid to move though my legs ached, lest I recall his attention to me too soon. At last he gave a sort of grunt, as if he had worked out to his satisfaction that I was not deceiving him.

'Very well, we will go,' he said. 'But no tricks, or you will regret it.'

I should have exulted in my victory, I suppose, but instead I felt as if I had sneaked up on the bull and got a very small piece of string around his horns and was preparing to lead him forth along the road. Now that he had made his decision, the big man became quite jolly. As we had an hour to spare, he insisted that I should sing some of the songs of Ireland for him. I tried to put him off, but he would have his way. Until now I had fancied myself quite a good singer. When the people gathered into our house of a winter's evening, they never got away without hearing at least two of my songs, and I had always found them an appreciative audience. But after that mad half-hour in the spidery kitchen, it was many a year before I allowed myself to be persuaded to sing for company again.

I began with 'Boulavogue', which was one of my favourites.

'Go on,' said Pietro stonily, when I had brought it to a wavering close, with tears in my eyes for the brave deeds of former times.

I followed that up with 'The Rising of the Moon' and 'Bold Robert Emmet' and 'Kelly of Killann'. Each time I finished, he told me in the same dead voice to start another. At the end of the fifth verse of 'Kelly of Killann' he said:

'Don't you know any songs without blood and fighting and killing in them? Don't you know any songs about love?'

I thought hard, and then I sang the ballad of Hugh Reynolds, written in Cavan gaol before he was hanged for abducting Catherine MacCabe. Then I sang one about a young man who mistook his true-love for a swan, as she sat under a tree, and who shot her. The last verse contains a warning.:

> *Now all you young fellows that carry a gun,*
> *Never go out shooting by the late setting sun.*
> *It might happen to others as it happened to me,*
> *To shoot your own true love all under a tree.*

I always used to sing with my eyes shut. I opened them now to find the big man almost snarling. He leaped out of his chair and strode up and down the kitchen.

'Do you call those two miserable wailings love-songs? It's just what I'd expect in a climate like this – misery and wailing. In Italy when we sing we are more cheerful.'

And he burst into a tremendous bellowing song, full of runs, and with a wonderful caressing chorus. He told me what the words said, that when the moon shines in a certain village on the bay of Naples, even the fish make love. Singing had put him in good humour, and he swung up and down the kitchen, raising the dust of the unswept floor and repeating the chorus of his song over and over.

While he was at this, the door opened silently. The small man had come down the stairs unheard by us, because of our concert. Now he stepped into the room, closing the door carefully behind him, and waited politely for Pietro to finish his song. He did not seem to see anything odd in the situation.

'Just in time, Miguel,' said the big man jovially. He slapped me on the shoulder, so that my knee-joints cracked. 'Here's Jim O'Malley, a nephew of our good friend Martin Walsh, come to take us away to a safer place.'

Miguel walked all around me, as if I had been a beast at a fair. Then he said some words in his own language. I could not understand them, but the contemptuous tone of Pietro's reply was unmistakable, and I felt myself go prickly with uneasiness. If I had even had Roddy by my side I should have felt more secure.

I hoped that Roddy had succeeded in his part of the plan. When he had finished talking to Pats Rua, he was to run like the wind back to Cloghanmore, cast off the *Saint Brendan* and sail her around to Uncle Martin's slip. There were many hazards to this plan. If by chance Pats Rua delayed him overlong, or if someone at Cloghanmore prevented him from boarding the *Saint Brendan*, it might be several hours before he would reach the slip. Then the tide or the wind might go against him, or he might find the boat too big for him to handle alone. He had assured me that this last was out of the question, but I knew that many a grown man would have thought twice about taking a hooker out alone in September seas. I would not even think of the possibility that the hooker might never arrive at all, and that I might be left with two furious men waiting vainly on the beach.

While I turned these unpleasant thoughts over in my mind, Miguel had been rolling various small objects in a piece of oil-skin. Among them I saw Pietro's fancy boots, which he had changed for the huge pair of sea-boots in which I had seen him land. I also saw the pair of bronze vases which had been the only ornaments in my uncle's drawing-room. Miguel held one of them up to the fading light to admire it, before putting it in with its fellow. No doubt the rest of the things were knick-knacks that they had picked up in other parts of the house.

'Now, Jim,' said Pietro heartily. 'You lead and we follow!'

And he went across and opened the back door with a flourish. I warned them to move very quietly, because the house was being watched. Then I walked out into the yard, with the two men on my heels. We stood for a second while the big man closed the door silently. Then we started up the yard for the gate.

8   Inishgower

At the gate I asked them to wait while I looked out on to the path. As far as I could see it was all quite still and peaceful. I signalled to the two men to follow me, and then I darted across the path of the low moss-covered stone wall that bordered the wood. I flung myself over the wall. They followed suit, and then we lay, all three of us, in a little hollow full of dry, tickling leaves, and listened. The wind mourned in the tree-tops above us, a doleful sound. With my ears strained to listen, gradually I began to hear other sounds – the wash of the waves on stones, the far-off bark of a dog, and the sudden clear call of a blackbird in another part of the wood. It was only when a robin hopped on to a stone within a few feet of us that I was sure we were not being quietly stalked. I began to move along on my stomach inside the wall, closely followed by my two silent companions.

Presently the trees thinned a little, and I knew we were coming near the shore. The wall was a little higher here and I stood up and stretched myself, glad not to be any longer on all fours, like a dog. Then I struck off through the trees, making straight for the seashore. It was well on in the afternoon by now, and the sun had disappeared into a bank of cloud, leaving a hard white light over the woods. Here near the sea the trees were evergreens, and they had a thin salt-bitten look, though they were tall and straight. They grew less closely too, and there was no underbrush, so that we were able to walk freely on the grass between. Now we could hear the sea quite plainly, and it sounded strangely with the thunder of the wind through the larches.

At the edge of the wood I was surprised to find a steep path leading down at an angle through big black rocks, to the shore. I had not known that there was a path here, for I had only come this way by chance. It was overgrown with rough sea-grass, so that it was easy to see that it was not much used. Uncle Martin did not look in the least like a seafaring man, and I could not imagine why he should need two separate ways to the sea.

I led our little procession along the path, which was almost like a ravine in places, so tall were the rocks on either side. Presently we came out on to a beach of white stones. I stopped to look about me. A hundred yards to my right was the slip, all quiet and deserted. Away off on my left a long green hill, cliff-faced to the sea, cut off my view of Cloghanmore village. While I watched, a pookawn rounded the cliff and came sailing towards us like a great black swan.

I pulled the two men into the shelter of the rocks at the end of the path and without a word we watched the boat's approach. The sea was smooth, with a swell that sent the boat up and down in long, slow curves. Her black sails were full, so that she tore along, sending a white wave streaming away from her bows. As she came closer I could make out a solitary figure in the stern.

'Here comes the *Saint Brendan*,' I said airily.

The two men seemed to accept this, for they made no reply. I hoped that I was right, and I watched the boat come closer and closer with such attention that by the time it was near enough to be recognised I saw a fleet of hookers all moving in unison.

It was the *Saint Brendan*, all right. As soon as it was opposite us, I stepped boldly out on to the shore. Roddy made no sign except to lift his hand once in a sort of salute. We hurried towards the slip, and were waiting there for some minutes before the boat slid slowly alongside and ground softly on the shallow bottom. I was in an agony until we had got the two men aboard, and had a foot of water between us and the slip. It was only then that I went back to the stern of the boat, where Roddy was handling the helm, to have a talk with him in Irish.

'How did you do it?' he asked at once.

'It was easy enough. They knew about me already, and I'd say they were tired of being barricaded into the house.'

'Did they ask you where you were taking them?'

'They don't seem very much interested. I suppose that is because they don't know this part of the world very well, and so one place is the same as another to them. I told them it is a place of safety.'

'It is, that,' said Roddy with a chuckle. 'They'll be safer than they bargain for.'

'I hope we'll be able to get them ashore,' I said uneasily. 'They came with us now like sheep, but if they don't see Uncle Martin when we land they may turn wicked.'

'You may be sure they will,' said Roddy.

'Isn't it a queer thing that there was no one watching the slip?' I said. 'I thought some of the Cloghanmore men would be there, and that we'd have to fight our way on to the *Saint Brendan*.'

'Jimmy Fagan was there,' said Roddy with a grin. 'I told Pats Rua that my father said he was to fetch Jimmy, and that the two of them were to go back to the big valley and see was it quiet there. I was afraid they would be back before I'd come with the boat, but we were in luck, it seems.'

While we were discussing our companions in our own language, they were discussing us in theirs. Now they came climbing along the length of the boat towards us, the little man behind the big man like a meadow pipit after a cuckoo.

'What is this place we are going?' the big man asked, and his face was full of suspicion.

'It is an island,' Roddy answered. 'We keep sheep there. The people from Cloghanmore never go there, so you will be quite safe.'

'Is Martin Walsh there now?'

'No, but he will come along later. That is the plan.'

It was our plan, but not Uncle Martin's.

'Are there no people on this island of yours?'

'No one, only a few sheep. There is a little house there. You will be quite comfortable.'

'What is to prevent us from taking this boat from you two boys now, and sailing her right back to Cloghanmore?'

'Nothing but your own good sense,' said Roddy. 'If you go back to Cloghanmore now, the people will make mincemeat of you.'

'They will, so,' said I confidently.

Pietro made no answer to this, but looked at us from under his eyebrows in a way that made me mighty uncomfortable. Then he sat on the end of the long seat that ran around the stern of the hooker, brooding and twisting his fingers in and out. Miguel got out a long knife and stropped it once or twice on a leather belt that he took from around his waist. Then he looked speculatively at my neck, as a farmer's wife might look at a turkey, coming on to Christmas. I put the big black sail between me and them as quickly as I could.

We followed the line of the shore for about a mile, past the big fertile valley with its little canals, and its lines of half-grown trees. We passed the end of the curving mountain range that sheltered it. A jumble of rocks ran out into the sea there, forming a long reef. We gave it a wide berth, and sailed around to the other side.

Then I saw the island. It was perhaps half a mile long, green on the lee side but sheeted with rock for the most part. Patches of green showed here and there among the rocks, and as we came close in I could see furiously nibbling sheep clinging to these little pastures. There was a tiny pier in a sheltered hollow, and the stone ruins of a house nearby showed that a family had lived here once. A little way up from the pier I could see a tiny shack, roughly thatched with rushes, which I guessed to be the little house that Roddy had mentioned. I knew there would be a bed of ferns there, and a stock of turf to build a fire with, so that the men would not come to any harm. I wondered if Roddy had thought of food for them.

Suddenly I realised that I was furiously hungry. I had had nothing to eat since breakfast, and now the blue day was fading, and the sea-air had sharpened my appetite so that the thought of food made me wince with longing. Roddy had had nothing either, so far as I knew, unless he had stopped in the village for some food before going down to the boat. Perhaps it was my hunger that left my courage so low, and that made me feel faint and sick at the thought of the task before us.

It was fortunate that we had a fair, clean breeze all the way to the island. It was more like a winter breeze than an autumn one, that clear, steady flow that we often get in frosty weather. Now that evening was coming on, there was a nip in the air, and a deep pink haze hung over the horizon. High above us I saw a feather of moon, although there was still plenty of daylight in the sky.

The sail came down with a creak and a rattle and then we slid in alongside the pier. Roddy hopped ashore and secured the boat by a single looped rope to the one bollard that was there. Then he called to us to come ashore too. Pietro stepped heavily on to the quay and then Miguel hopped up beside him like a bird. I was the last to leave the boat, and by the time I was ashore the others were already on their way up the track to the house. I did not hurry to catch up with them, for I could hear Pietro questioning Roddy closely about Uncle Martin. He wanted to know where Uncle Martin was now, and how soon he was coming to the island, and where they would go after that. Roddy answered him confidently, saying that Uncle Martin would be along soon, and that we were only boys and must do as we were told. I thought that the big man was beginning to doubt our innocence, for he gave Roddy a sharp sideways look at this last statement. Still he did not pause in his swinging walk, and within a few minutes we had reached the house.

The door was held with a simple hasp, which Roddy unhooked. Then he pushed the door in and stood aside for the men to enter. This time Miguel trotted in first, like a curious dog, and Pietro followed more slowly, bending his head under the lintel. Roddy followed them in, but I stood on the door-stone, just outside.

'You see, it's a fine house,' said Roddy. 'There's a grand heap of ferns to sleep on, and we'll have a fire going in two shakes.'

He went over to the pile of turf by the fireplace, and built a wall of turf-sods on the hearth. He got a few handfuls of soft dry turf, placed them against his wall and lit them. Then he put more turf around the front and stood back to watch the grey smoke curling in a thickening stream up the chimney.

'There, now,' he said in a satisfied tone. 'You'll be quite comfortable here until we come back.'

'Until you come back?' Pietro said sharply. 'Oh, no! You're not going to leave us so easily.'

It was Roddy's speed that saved us. He shot out of the door as if from a spring, nearly knocking me sprawling where I stood. By the time I had recovered my balance he had the flimsy hasp on the door, and then we streaked down the track towards the boat, as fast as ever a hare ran at a coursing match.

We were no more than half-way there when the door burst open. The two men came pounding after us, shouting wildly. We did not look back. I cannot remember covering the last few yards. Perhaps I flew. Roddy twitched the rope off the bollard and we leaped into the boat. With panting breath and hot, shaking hands we pushed the *Saint Brendan* along the quay wall, until she sailed free. There were eight feet of water between us and the land when the two men reached the quay. We were hauling on the sheets and raising the big black sail, and moving foot by foot away from them.

I saw Pietro measure the distance with his eye, as if he thought of jumping aboard. He might have succeeded, because of his great size, had not Miguel distracted his attention. The little man had got up on a jutting rock, and taken aim, and now he sent his newly stropped knife flying through the air after us. His aim was good. I felt a stinging pain in my arm, as my

left coat sleeve was pinned to the mast. Startled, Pietro paused just too long, and then we were out of reach.

Since then I have often admired my own presence of mind, justly, I think. I got my right arm around and pulled out the knife, coolly wiped my own blood off it and stuck it in my belt. I took no notice of the warm trickle that ran down my arm, though I knew I would have to attend to it as soon as we would be out of sight. I saw Roddy's eyes light up with admiration of my courage, and was sufficiently rewarded.

You may be sure that we were glad to sit down in the stern of the *Saint Brendan* and recover our breath and our wits. Roddy found a little roll of bandage with which to tie up my arm. He said that even Uncle Martin had the sense to keep some in the boat, in case anyone were injured while she was at sea. I asked him when he had decided to make a run for it.

'I thought of that just as we landed,' he said. 'I said to myself that we could be persuading them until midnight, and maybe be kept prisoner after all our trouble, so the less talk we had the better.'

'It worked, all right,' said I.

'It very nearly didn't,' said Roddy, and suddenly we both felt very weary.

'Roddy,' I said after a moment. 'I could eat a dozen of those fine fat seagulls that are following us.'

'There's no need for that,' he said. 'Anyway, you'd probably do better to take a bite out of the side of the boat. Seagulls are made of black rubber, flavoured with fish.'

While he spoke he was reaching in under the seat, where he had a brown-paper parcel. He lashed the helm, and then we opened the parcel. There was a long loaf of shop bread, and a thick slice of cooked ham. We had no butter, but there were no complaints on that score. I do not know what they eat in heaven, but it could not be more wonderful than that meal.

We worked hard at our task and neither of us spoke until we had finished everything. I chased a crumb that lay concealed under a fold of paper, and then we sat back and enjoyed the feeling of being well-filled again. After a moment I said:

'Where did you get the good food?'

'I stopped at Paddy Conneeley's shop on my way through Cloghanmore,' he said. 'I knew we'd have to get food somewhere, and I was afraid it would be a long time before we would get the chance again. Paddy wasn't there – he had gone into the kitchen, I suppose, or into the parlour where the meeting was still going on. I could hear them talking away in there, cross like, and someone was thumping the table. Anyway, there wasn't a sinner in the shop, so I got the big loaf out of the bread-bin and I whacked a lump of ham off the piece on the counter. My father can pay Paddy later on.'

'It was a good chance,' I said, with feeling.

I really believed I would have died of hunger before we could get home, if it had not been for Roddy's presence of mind. Suddenly a thought struck me.

'What will the foreign men eat on the island?'

'They'll be all right,' said Roddy carelessly. 'There's a bag of spuds in the corner of the house, and a good spring well of water to boil them with, out at the back.'

'But will they think of boiling spuds?' I asked. 'I hear that they don't go in for them at all in foreign countries, the way we do.'

'They'll think of them when they get hungry enough,' said Roddy. 'The like of those fellows always make out enough to eat. If they want stronger meat, they can kill a sheep. I bet you fourpence they'll think of that. And they can milk a sheep, too, if they like.'

'Sheep's milk wouldn't be my own fancy,' I said.

I said no more about the plight of the foreigners, however, for Roddy had convinced me that they would survive until our return.

'What will happen if the people they are expecting come in a boat and take them away?'

'Won't we be delighted if they do?' said Roddy heartily. 'I'd say that if they get away from that island they won't be in all that of a hurry to come back to Cloghanmore. If he was all alone, we'd make short work of your Uncle Martin.'

Then he looked at me uneasily, lest I might take offence, but I was long past that now.

We had decided to bring the *Saint Brendan* back to Cloghanmore quay, in the hope that she would not have been missed. It would have been quicker, perhaps, to have gone straight back to Uncle Martin's slip with her, and from there to the house in the tree. But we could not hope again for such luck as we had had the last time. If Pats and Jimmy Fagan were back from their tour of the valley, we could easily be delayed so long that our plan would be spoiled.

It was really dusk by the time we reached the quay. Lights showed in all the houses, and the people's voices talking to each other from door to door were carried to us clearly on the frosty air. We slipped in among the other boats and tied the *Saint Brendan* up to the quay wall. Roddy was up the ladder first. With my foot on the lowest rung to follow him, I heard a voice challenge him:

'So it's yourself, Roddy Faherty! And where might you be coming from?'

Roddy did not answer for a moment, and I guessed that he had been surprised. I did not stir. Then I heard Roddy say:

'My father told me to take the *Saint Brendan* around by Cloghanmore House and see was there any strange boats out that way.'

'Did he, now?' said the other, disbelievingly. 'This is the first I heard of it. It's a wonder he didn't tell me that he was sending you. And how smart you were, to slip down and sail the pookawn away without a word to me! I've had forty fits since I found she was gone.'

'You should have been minding her better,' said Roddy slyly.

'I should so,' said the other disconsolately. 'And that's the second time that boat disappeared when my back was turned. Don't tell your father at all that you got away with her so easy.'

'I won't say a word,' said Roddy solemnly.

'Good boy, good boy.' He sounded relieved. 'Did you see any strange boats?'

'I did not,' said Roddy, and then he went on in an aggrieved tone: 'And I'm thinking my father knew right well that there were no boats to be seen, and that he only wanted to get me out of the way. You'd think I wasn't a grown man, as big as himself, the way he goes on!'

The man laughed, convinced by this that Roddy was telling the truth.

'Your father is above at Paddy Conneeley's shop still,' he said. 'There's going to be great work here tonight, by the sound of things. And my own case is as bad as yours, for I was given the job of watching the quay, a couple of miles away from where all the fun will be.'

I judged that it would be safe to come ashore now, and I climbed the ladder and stood beside Roddy. His companion was a lively man of about forty, I thought, though I could not see him properly in the dark. He knew me at once, however, and he shuffled from foot to foot with embarrassment for me, because of my wicked uncle. He was delighted to see us leave him.

Roddy chuckled to himself as soon as we were out of hearing.

'That was Nedeen Cleary,' he said. 'Fighting and crossness don't suit him at all, for all his talk.' He was silent for a moment and then he said suddenly: 'Oh, Jim, amn't I a terrible liar?'

'You are that,' said I sardonically. 'You should have told him that we had just abducted the two foreigners and were coming back now for Uncle Martin.'

He laughed.

'Sure, I know I couldn't do that,' he said. 'But I do get frightened at the way the lies roll out of me, so sweet and easy they'd nearly deceive St Peter. You'd think I had plenty of practice at it.'

I tried to console him by saying that as soon as this adventure was over he could make up his mind to stick to the sober truth for the rest of his life.

'That's the trouble,' he said mournfully. 'By that time the habit will have grown on me. And besides, I'm noticing that I *like* telling lies! Isn't that an awful thing?'

'It's all that,' said I, 'and you'll come to a bad end if you go the way you're going!'

But he didn't like that either. Fortunately we were in the village by this time, so we had to stop talking.

Now that we knew that the men were still conferring in Paddy Conneeley's shop, we decided not to delay in the village at all. We guessed that they were waiting for the dead black night to fall. This gave us a little time to complete our work, if we were able.

'But we must hurry,' said Roddy. 'If Nedeen tells my father that I was out in the *Saint Brendan*, my father will know at once that we're up to something. That man could see through a stone wall, I'd swear,' he added, with a mixture of admiration and irritation.

We went along the shore, climbing over the weedy rocks and slipping into unexpected pools, until we had left the village behind. Then we came out on the main road again, and set off at a jog-trot for the Cloghanmore woods. We did not speak, for we needed all our breath. That piece of ground that I had travelled so often in the last two days seemed to me the most wearisome corner of the whole wide world. We paused only once, to see Roddy's horse grazing comfortably in the field in which we had left him. He lifted his head and whinnied to us, and Roddy whinnied back. The very last of the daylight faded as we turned down towards the sea again. By the time we reached the edge of the wood it was pitch dark.

After my recent experiences, I fancied myself an expert at working my way through dark woods. Perhaps I had really learned how to do it. With considerable pride, I found that I

had no trouble in leading the way to the clearing where Uncle
Martin's house was.

We paused under the tree. The wind had dropped with the
fall of night. We listened, and I fancied that I could hear a little
scuffling sound up there. I felt about for the trailing ivy stem
and silently pulled the ladder down. Then, like a couple of
prowling cats, we climbed up into the tree.

We left the ladder hanging, so as not to make any delay.
Holding on to each other in the deep blackness, we felt our way
over to the mat that covered the doorway of the house. Then,
with a sudden movement, I twitched it aside and we both darted
into the house together.

I dropped the mat instantly into place, and we stood there,
staring. Uncle Martin stood at the far side of the little room and
stared back at us. Two candles, standing on the box in the
middle of the floor, gave enough light to see by. His face was as
still as a mask, and for more than a minute he did not move·
Then he cleared his throat with that little chirping sound that
I had come to hate, and said peevishly:

'So you came back, at last. Where have you been?'

'Risking my life for you and your tricks,' I said boldly.

His eyes hardened at once, and for all his small size and his
miserable little body, for one moment he looked as dangerous
as a snake.

'Did anything happen to you?' he asked contemptuously.
'And who is your friend?'

'If anything happened to me, you wouldn't lose any sleep,' I
said. 'I've heard the whole story of what happened in these
parts.'

He raised his eyebrows, but made no reply except to ask me
again to introduce him to my friend.

'My name is Roddy Faherty,' said Roddy quietly. 'You ought
to know me, for you know my father, John Faherty, very well
indeed.'

'So I do, so I do,' said Uncle Martin, and shifted his eyes

from ours. There was a pause, and then he gave a long windy sigh. 'Well, Jim, I waited all night for you,' he said then. 'I made sure at last that you must have gone back to your mother, and I could not find it in my heart to blame you. Why should you want to help me, when your mother had poisoned your mind against me, this many a year.'

And he fetched another sigh.

'My mother hardly ever mentioned you,' I said hotly. 'I told you so last night.'

'Did you? Well my memory is not what it was. Why were you so ready to believe all that my good neighbours have said about me, then?'

'Are you saying that you never robbed the people of Cloghanmore?' Roddy demanded.

'I was only taking charge of their money,' he pleaded. 'I didn't mean any harm. You can both go away now and tell them that they'll get their money back, soon. Yes, very soon.'

And he took a step forward, as if to hustle us out of the house. Roddy moved to meet him, threateningly.

'It would be fitter for you to admit what you did,' he said angrily. ''Tis an awful thing to see an old man able to tell such lies.' Neither of us saw any humour in this. Roddy went on: 'I wonder will you change your tune when you hear that your two foreign friends are gone.'

'Gone! They're not gone! Jim, Jim! Are they gone?'

I nodded. The change that came over him then was almost pathetic. He ran from one of us to the other two or three tiny steps each time, asking us where the foreigners had gone, and whether the Cloghanmore people knew that he was still in the district. We told him that we had captured his two friends ourselves and deposited them on Inishgower, and we added that he had been seen this morning crossing from the wood to the house. He almost wept at that, and he kept on saying that he was a wicked old man, and must say his prayers. He was a horrible sight, and I was relieved when Roddy interrupted him.

'We have really come to help you,' he said. 'If you will give us back the money, we can promise you that the people will let you go free. They don't want to injure you. They only want their rights.'

He nodded several times, and then he had a long fit of the shivers. Time was passing, and we were becoming uneasy lest the Cloghanmore men might arrive at the house before we would have persuaded him. I added my voice to Roddy's, urging him to lead us to the place where he had hidden the money. At last he said wearily:

'Very well. I will do that. I'm beaten. The money is in Clog-hanmore House.'

And he dropped his head on his chest as if his scraggy neck were broken. Roddy and I looked at each other in triumph.

9 The priest's room

Now that Uncle Martin had agreed to return the money we were impatient to make him do so at once. Still we did not want to hurry him too much, lest he might change his mind. A strange, wild light had come into his eyes, as if he were on the verge of madness, with disappointment at his failure. If we drove him too hard, I thought, he might cross the border into real insanity, and be quite unable to lead us to the place where he had hidden the money.

So we bore with him while he questioned us about the two foreigners. He wanted to know how we had managed to deceive them, and whether we had been afraid of them, and whether they had tried to fight us. We answered in a general way, without telling exactly what had happened. You may be sure we gave no details of the state of terror which we had endured until the men were safely on the island. I mentioned that Miguel had thrown his knife at us, and I showed him the bandage on my arm and the knife in my belt to prove it.

'But of course these little things are not important,' I said carelessly.

He looked at me with increased respect, I thought, and I felt myself swell with pride.

At this point Roddy judged that it would be safe to say:

'We had better hurry, Mr Walsh. We must have the money ready to give to the Cloghanmore men as soon as they come. You can stay out of sight until we have handed it over, and we will make them promise not to hurt you.'

Uncle Martin cast down his eyes at this, and I guessed that he was humiliated at receiving such a promise from a boy. Roddy noticed the same thing, and the two of us strutted like turkey-cocks over our unfortunate victim. We would have been better occupied in thinking over his former treachery, and in remembering that criminals do not usually repent and change their ways in a matter of minutes, and at the persuasion of two country boys. We had plenty of time to think of this later.

'Come along, then,' said Roddy roughly, and went to blow out the candles.

Uncle Martin put one of the candles in his pocket, to light us around the house, he said. I reached for the other, and slipped it into my own pocket, thinking that it might turn in useful. Then we led the old man out of the house on to the platform, one on either side of him, for we were not entirely dead to the possibility of his trying to escape. I went down the ladder first. Then came Uncle Martin, agile as a monkey for all his years. I grasped him by the elbow, and I could not help feeling sorry for him as I felt his little bones through his coat-sleeve. Roddy came last, and then Uncle Martin insisted that we haul up the ladder. We were not inclined to delay, but he twittered and chirped so fiercely that we felt it would be safer to please him in this.

Still keeping him between us, we found the path to the house. At the edge of the wood we paused. Roddy explained that we must make a run for it, in order to get across the path and into the yard unseen. I prayed that some zealous person would not interfere now, just as we were on the point of success.

'Yes, yes, I understand,' Uncle Martin whispered.

There was just enough moonlight to light up our way. I wished there had been less, for it would show us all too clearly as we flitted across. However, there was nothing to be done about this, so we grasped our prisoner and trotted him briskly over to the deep shadow alongside the house. There we paused to listen. There were faint night noises which could have been made equally well by the midges or by an army moving into position. After a second we moved off again towards the gate into the yard. The shadows were comforting, but we did not feel safe until we were inside the yard gate. A minute later we were standing in the dark kitchen, where Pietro and I had so recently entertained each other with songs.

We had placed all our faith in our guess that the Cloghan-more men would not have occupied the house since last I had left it. For all they knew, Pietro and Miguel were still inside, waiting anxiously for reinforcements from the sea. At this thought I gasped. I had forgotten all about those reinforcements. Perhaps they were on their way to the house now. Perhaps they were already inside. I vented my fright on Uncle Martin.

'Hurry up!' I said roughly, pushing him towards the door. 'Lead us to the money at once, or it will be the worse for you!'

He shook off my hand.

'I'm in as much of a hurry as you are,' he said angrily. 'Do you think I enjoy your company?'

He struck a light and put it to his candle, and I could see his ill-tempered little mouth screwed up with hatred of me. He started for the door.

'This time I'll go first,' he said over his shoulder. 'It will do the two of you good to follow, for once.'

And he trotted out into the passage. We almost had to run to keep up with him. He followed the stone passage-way towards the front of the house, and presently he paused by a door to our right. We came up with him there, and he made me hold the candle while he took down a heavy bar that kept the door shut. I thought it a strange thing to see a barred door inside a house. Then he fumbled in his pocket and took out a big key, and un-locked the door, which swung outwards on creaking hinges. Without a word he seized the candle from my hand and trotted before us into the room. We followed more slowly.

It was a small room, bare of furniture except for a single low press that stood against one wall. There was but one high win-

113

dow, and a tall narrow fireplace with a flagged hearth. It looked as if it might have been an office or a business room at one time. Uncle Martin placed the candle on top of the press and again fumbled in his pocket for the keys. Roddy took the candle in his hand and held it in readiness, so that it would shine into the press the moment that it would be opened. Almost at bursting point with impatience, I walked nervously to the fireplace.

What happened then was so fast that I have never really got the rights of it. We had left the door standing open. The next thing I knew was that Uncle Martin was outside that door, and had slammed it shut. A second too late we came to life. Roddy dropped the candle. We charged across the room. At the same moment our bodies crashed against the door, a short second too late. The big bar had slipped into place. Outside the door, we heard Uncle Martin patter off down the corridor, giggling.

I almost burst into tears of rage and disappointment. Beside me, Roddy was deadly silent, as if he too were wrestling with tears. Suddenly I gave one thump of the door with my fist.

'Don't waste your strength, Jim,' said Roddy dully. 'We deserve this for being so cocksure.'

It was a humiliating moment for us, there in the dark, with the tables so suddenly and surely turned upon us. Now we were able to see that he had given in too easily. Now we knew that boys are helpless creatures, for all their pretence of manliness. I felt as if I were about five years old. At last Roddy broke the silence that had fallen between us.

'Ah, well, it's no use brooding anyway,' he said. 'Our first business is to get out of this place.'

He lit a match and found the candle, and lit it. I felt myself grow a little more cheerful, with the light.

'We can get out by the window,' I said.

We lifted the press over to the wall under the window. While we carried it, its doors swung slowly open. It was completely empty. It had not been locked at all. I laughed at our innocence, but Roddy did not seem to see much humour in the business.

115

'If we don't get free before my father comes along to burn down the house, it will be a poor lookout for us,' he said, effectively destroying my rising spirits.

This was a truly horrid thought, and one that had slipped my mind. It certainly had the effect that Roddy wanted, of making me concentrate on the business of our escape.

He held the press steady while I climbed up. I found that my chin was on the level of the window-sill. Though the window was small, it looked big enough to let us climb through. Suddenly I struck out with my bare hand and smashed the glass. Then I dropped my bleeding hand by my side. I remember that my voice shook with the effort to keep it from sounding hysterical as I said:

'Roddy, this window is bricked up.'

He would not believe me at first. He had to climb up beside me and see and feel it for himself. Then he said:

'Well, if that doesn't beat all! From below it looks just like an ordinary window. Of course, with the candlelight, and it being night-time –'

'Uncle Martin is no fool,' I said, and it was the first time I had accorded him any respect.

After that, we indulged in feeling foolish for a while. It was no wonder that we had thought our escape by way of the window would be easy, for the glass and frame had been left in position when the window was bricked up. But now we knew that Uncle Martin was far too clever to have put us into a room which it would be so easy to escape; and this knowledge was, for us, the beginning of wisdom. Until now we had thought ourselves very clever fellows, able to get ourselves out of any predicament. This had made us foolhardy, and now it looked as if we were going to pay dear for our boldness. One thought brought me a little consolation, as we returned to the middle of the room.

'Perhaps Uncle Martin intends to ransom us for the money,' I said.

But the thought of being treated like a kidnapped baby made Roddy's blood boil.

'Faith and soul, he won't ransom me!' he said venomously. 'Long, long before I'll be the cause of him getting away with what he stole!'

He seized me by the shoulder and gazed into my eyes with a long searching look.

'Jim,' he said. 'Have you courage?'

'I always thought I had,' said I disconsolately, 'but now I don't know.'

'I'll help you,' he said. 'Call up what courage you have left, for you're going to need it now. We're going to climb that chimney.'

I looked across at the narrow grate, and said:

'I'd rather die here.'

But he insisted and argued and persuaded me until I had to agree to try it.

'We are locked in here,' he said. 'There is only the one way out. We must take it.'

'But it's so narrow and black. We'll suffocate, we'll die up there.'

He said he would go first, and that he was bigger than I was, and would be able to warn me if it was getting too narrow. I knew I was mean to be comforted with this, and I wondered if I would ever have had the heroism to go first myself.

We each tore a strip off the tail of our shirts, with which to bandage our noses and mouths against the soot. Then Roddy took the candle over and held it up the chimney as high as he could. It was an advantage that the chimney was so narrow, he said, for we could do without footholds by pressing our knees apart against the walls. He withdrew his head so that I could look, and stopped at the sight of my white face and staring eyes.

'Jim, you can stay here,' he said quickly. 'As soon as I get out, I'll come around by the door and set you free.'

117

But I had made up my mind to go, and I had gone numb in the head from fear of it. I was not even capable of changing my mind. I said I was going with him, and that we should start at once.

He blew out the candle and put it in his pocket without another word. Then I heard him scramble about for his first foot-hold in the chimney. I heaved him up from below and felt his feet dangle against my face. A whisper came from above:

'It's quite easy.'

A strange thing was that once the candle was quenched a great deal of my horror of the chimney was gone. Once I was in the dark already, the darkness of the chimney was no hardship. I soon found, too, that either I was narrower than I had thought, or the chimney was wider. It was many a year since a fire had been lit in the grate, and the soot was packed hard on the chimney walls, so as to make admirable footholds. All the loose soot had long since fallen down, no doubt. Roddy's whispers of encouragement from above me helped to keep me from despair, but although the whole business was better than I had expected I shall never forget it the longest day I live.

Presently I began to wonder what we would do when we would get to the top. There would be a chimney-pot there, and it would narrow off. Panic swept over me. Just then Roddy's voice came again:

'I've come to a ledge up here, Jim. I'll wait for you.'

He reached down a hand to me, and helped me up beside him. It was wonderful to sit there in the dark and feel secure for a few minutes. We were on a sort of stone shelf, set in the chimney wall. I could not imagine what its purpose could have been. Roddy suggested that it might have been made by workmen when they were building the house, to rest their buckets of mortar on, perhaps. We felt around with our hands and discovered that it was not merely a rough shelf of rock. It was made of carefully cut stone, in blocks, fitted neatly together and pointed with mortar. We talked about the strangeness of that for a while, to keep our minds occupied. All at once I felt a shiver go through me, and then a second one. I could not stop them. They came one after another, shaking me miserably, and leaving me each time more spent and exhausted. I was bitterly ashamed of myself, but I was quite unable to control them. I do not know what would have become of us, had not Roddy grasped my arm and said:

'Jim! I think there is a passageway of some sort behind us. I've been feeling with my hands.'

I made some reply between my chattering teeth. Roddy sprang up behind me and hauled me backwards by the shoulders. Then he talked to me for a while. I remember trying to tell him that he should leave me, and finding that I could not make him understand. At last he said:

'Just lie here, Jim, until I come back. I'm going to find out where this passageway goes.'

The strange thing was that I was quite at peace while he was gone. I stopped shivering and lay still, with my limbs relaxed and my eyes shut against the dark. It was almost as if I were dead, I thought, and I got a queer pleasure from the idea. I think it was the sensation of complete despair.

Still I came to myself quickly enough when I heard Roddy's excited whisper as he came crawling back towards me:

'Jim! The queerest thing you ever saw in all your born days! Get up, quick, and come and see it!'

The idea of seeing anything was enough for me. I followed him in the darkness by the sense of hearing, and by the feel of the passage walls. It was a narrow, low-roofed place, and we had to go on all fours. A draught from somewhere blew fresh air around us, so that we were no longer breathing soot. The stones felt soft under my hands, as if they were covered with a drift of dust.

A yard or two from where I had lain, waiting for Roddy, the passage took a little turn, and then I saw a faint pink light ahead.

'Quiet!' Roddy hissed over his shoulder.

I strangled the shout that had almost escaped me. Now I could see the vague outline of Roddy moving slowly ahead of me. Then I saw him stand up, so that only his legs were visible to me. It was a moment before I understood that the passage had ended, and that he had reached a little room in which he now stood waiting for me.

Like a tortoise looking out of his shell, I crouched on all fours at the mouth of the passage and stared around in bewilderment. Roddy moved a step or two away, to give me room to crawl out slowly and stand in the middle of the floor. It was a tiny vaulted room, perhaps six feet either way, built of the same dressed stone that we had recognised by the feel on the chimney ledge. The faint light came from a hole in the stone floor at one side. Smoke came up through the same hole, and went out by another one in the ceiling. A low stone coping had been built on the floor of our little room, edging the hole, to direct the smoke upward. Roddy came close to me and breathed ticklingly into my ear.

'It's smoke from the drawing-room fire.'

Now I remembered the wide, cavernous chimney of the drawing-room, with its little ashy fire, and Fursey, the cat, sitting calmly in front of it. I remembered how he had called lazily to me through the door, and I wondered where he was now.

Grasping my elbow, Roddy led me across to the chimney. Noiselessly we knelt on the floor and cautiously looked over the coping. A sudden sideways puff of smoke shot into our faces. Tears blinded me, and I leaned back with my fists to my eyes. Presently I had recovered, and I bent forward again. I saw that Roddy had been in the same predicament. With our heads together we looked down the chimney into the fire.

It was like looking into the crater of a volcano. We could see right into the red heart of the fire, in its ring of black turf-sods. A little piece of the flagged hearth was visible too, and while we watched Fursey walked stealthily across. I guessed that there was a lamp in the room too, for there was more light than could have come from the fire.

Suddenly, with a little scurry of turf-dust, the cat trotted across the hearth again. Then my heart gave a dreadful bound. From below came a little querulous chirping cough. I grasped Roddy's arm. We crouched, as still as death. No one but my uncle could have made that sound. He was in the room below us, at this moment. If there had been any doubt in our minds, it was not long before it was removed. Up the chimney came the sound of Uncle Martin's voice. He was talking to the cat.

'Heh, heh!' came his queer little laugh. 'I settled those two prowlers, Fursey, my boy. Oh, yes! I fixed them.' Now we could hear him shuffle quickly across the room. 'Just one or two things to be done now, and we can be off. Yes, yes, you're coming with me of course, of course.'

There was a lot more, but we could not hear every word. From time to time he gave a little excited giggle, as if he were really pleased with his evening's work. I felt my legs go stiff with cramp. We were afraid to move lest he might hear us. A tickling had started in my throat, too, which I feared would turn into a cough at any moment. It was the soot, which had a loathsome taste. The tickling became worse with every moment, until I thought my lungs must burst with the effort not to cough. I clutched at Roddy so that he thought I was fainting. Another minute of this and I must surely give way.

But now, like a lifebuoy to a drowning man, came the sound of the door opening. Uncle Martin was going away. Until the door shut behind him I held my breath, and then I let it out in a cough that shook the soot out of the chimney with a soft rustle into the fire. With the closing of the door another puff of smoke had come up the chimney, so that Roddy began to cough too. We were like two sheepdogs barking after a contrary flock on the mountainside.

It was now that we made the strangest discovery of all. Afterwards it fascinated me to think that but for my fit of coughing we might never have found it at all. In order to get as far as possible from the chimney, we had gone back to the farthest end of the room. The dust that lay everywhere moved in a little cloud around our feet, making the dimness even more obscure. Leaning helplessly against the wall, I was the first to see the bag.

It was a small, strong canvas bag, of the kind that I know now is used by banks for sending large amounts of money. Of course we did not recognise it for what it was then, because neither of us had ever set foot in a bank. What struck me first was that it was a sign that people other than ourselves had been in this room. Then I observed that the bag was new. This meant that someone had been here very recently indeed. Now Roddy had seen it too, and together we knelt down to examine it.

It stood neatly in the corner, leaning against the wall. It was not very heavy, for it was packed mostly with paper money. There were some small paper bags of coins as well, but most of it was in notes. We cut the string at the neck of the bag, and felt them with our hands. Then we sat back on our heels and stared at it silently.

At last Roddy said softly:

'Jim, this means that Martin Walsh knows about this hidey-hole. He was telling the truth when he said that the money was in Cloghanmore House.'

'He should have been a rat,' I said sourly. 'He has a great fancy for hidey-holes.'

'Now if he goes to see that we are still safely locked up,' Roddy went on, 'he'll surely come here at once to make sure that his money is safe.'

'He won't go to look at us,' I said uneasily.

'Even if he does not, he'll come here,' said Roddy. 'Didn't you hear him telling the old cat that he would be leaving the house soon? We'll have to get down that chimney as quickly as possible, and that little bag must come too.'

I knew this was sense, but my insides withered at the thought of dropping down the chimney into heaven knew what new dangers. We crossed the room again, to look down into the fire. I had thought that the senses of surprise and fright must be worn out in me now. But I think that the worst point in the whole business was what came next.

A whirling, and a scrabbling, and a clawing began in the chimney below us. We drew back. In the dim light I could see that Roddy's face was green. Nearer and nearer came the scratching. Then Fursey's head came up over the coping. He climbed up and stood there stiffly, his tail erect, and his big round eyes like lamps shining expressionlessly.

He turned his head from Roddy to me, and back again. We stared back at him. He crouched, as if he were going to spring at us and tear us.

'Pish-wish,' said I weakly, conciliatingly.

He spat at us forcefully, and with the utmost contempt. It was almost as if he had said:

'Pish-wish, yourself!'

Then, with flying tail and a quick twist of his body, he sprang down the chimney again. We leaned quickly over the coping and saw him cling, once, to the chimney wall, and then drop accurately beyond the fire. Then we heard him trotting about the room, in that thumping way that cats have, miawing loudly.

'The devil is in that cat,' said Roddy sourly. 'Can't you hear him calling Martin Walsh?'

We were both annoyed with ourselves for having been so frightened by a cat, and I think this helped us over the next part. Roddy had string in his pocket, and we made a kind of harness for him, to which I tied the bag, so that it hung on his back. He would need his two hands free for climbing down the chimney. It was slow and difficult work, there in the dim light, and with my hands sweaty and shaking with nervousness. But at last I had it done. I pulled at the bag to make sure that it would not fall off while he was on his way down the chimney.

Now that the time had come to go down, we found that there would be no question of climbing. We were not cats, to cling by our nails to rough stone walls that sloped away from under us. I went first, because Roddy was burdened with the money.

I swung myself over the coping, keeping as much as possible to one side, for I did not fancy dropping into the fire. While I hung there by my hands. I could feel its threatening heat on the soles of my bare feet. It was an effort to let go, and it was a full minute before I could force myself to do it. Roddy said not a word, though he might have been urging me to hurry. When at last I did drop, I tried to twitch my body sideways as it fell, as I had seen the porpoises do on a summer evening as they jumped and played behind a boat. I was not as muscular as a porpoise, but I did not do too badly. I cleared the fire, at any rate, though I landed in the hot ashes, which sent me dancing into the middle of the room.

Fursey scratched at my heels like a dog while I went to help Roddy. I kicked at him, and he sank his teeth in me. I declare that he was the strangest cat I ever encountered. Roddy dropped almost in the same spot that I had, and I steadied him with my hand until he found his balance. Then we rushed to the window.

Fursey cried and called around the door while we flung the shutters back and forced the window up. Heaven knows how long it was since last it had been opened. Paint cracked and spiders scurried while we worked at it, and at last we were able to slip outside. I almost became drunk with my first mouthful of fresh air and freedom. Fursey sprang on to the window-sill to stare after us, while the lamp flared high in the draught behind him. We flashed around the corner of the house and a moment later we were in the woods.

10 Anna Faherty takes command

Once we were safely in the woods the whole adventure that we had just been through appeared like a lunatic dream. It hardly seemed possible that it was we who had been shut into a room, and had escaped by the chimney, and had found a bag of money in a priest's hole. It was the sort of adventure that might have befallen one of those strange nerveless heroes of ancient Ireland, who would undertake a trip to the Land of Youth as calmly as I would start out for Westport fair. Even now, the horror of the dark chimney was still upon us. Neither of us wanted to talk about it lest we might live through the nightmare again. The only comment was made by Roddy.

'If I were at home in my own place this minute,' he whispered, 'I wouldn't call the Queen my aunt.'

I thought of the bright kitchen with its photographs of the relations in America and its shining, rosy delph. Back across the wood we went, under the house in the tree without an upward glance, until we reached the boundary wall by the shore. Here where the trees were thinner, there was a searching little wind, strong enough to make the branches sing a mournful song overhead, in unison with the heavy song of the waves. We stopped to listen, but nothing could be heard above that concert. After a moment I climbed over the wall and walked a few paces away. If anyone were watching I would surely be challenged, and while I would hold the watcher in talk, Roddy could slip off out of the wood by another way.

No one called out to me to halt, and after a moment I went

125

back and told Roddy that it was safe to come out. Afterwards we discovered that we had escaped the sentry by a few yards.

Once out in the open Roddy took the lead. He bounded along like a hare in high grass, so that it was all I could do to keep up with him. He had unharnessed the bag from his shoulders, and he grasped its neck tightly while he ran. Presently we were making our way up along the bed of the stream. The cold water on our feet was a delight. We dared not pause for a drink at the well, but hurried up the little lane to the corner field where we could see the tall shape of the horse waiting at the gate. He shook his head at us and whinnied reproachfully.

'Faith and I don't know what *you* have to complain about,' said Roddy, as he slipped the straddle to the ground.

He and the horse rubbed noses in a most friendly fashion. Then he went on:

'Now maybe you'll take us home, sir, if you please!'

The horse edged his hind quarters around towards us, as if to say that we were welcome. He was a tall horse, and we had to climb on the gate to get on his back. Roddy sat in front and took the reins. I held the bag with one hand and Roddy's belt with the other. Then we started out on to the main road as soberly as if we had been a man and his wife on their way to church on a Sunday morning. Though it was no more than nine o'clock we did not see a soul on the way, neither on the main road nor in the boreens. We kept a sharp eye open at every corner, where on any other evening we would certainly have seen a crowd of men lying in the shelter of the wall.

'I don't like it,' said Roddy softly. 'I'd like to know what they're up to. I'd like to know where my father is, and Scoot, and all the rest of them.'

We were on high ground now, and we looked down at the Cloghanmore woods. It was all black and silent there. Not even a speck of light showed. We had left the shutters open and the light streaming out across the gravel. It seemed as if Uncle Martin must have returned to the drawing-room and found the window open. Then he would have quenched the lamp and gone in search of us. In imagination I saw him wrench open the door of our prison, and then go fluttering all over the house looking for us, like a malignant bat. I wondered if he would then climb into the secret room to see if his bag of stolen money were safe. But I could not imagine what he would do after he had discovered that it was gone. With all my heart I hoped that he would become frightened, and that he would sneak out of the house and away from the district while there was yet time.

'We should have left a letter for Uncle Martin,' I said. 'We could have told him that we had taken the money and that he should leave the country as quickly as he could –'

'A fat lot of time we had for writing letters,' Roddy interrupted me. 'And we had no pen and paper. If you're still worrying about your uncle's skin, I suppose we'll have to go back and get him safely away as soon as we have put this little haul of ours in my mother's keeping.'

I said nothing. I think that one word from me would have been enough to make Roddy abandon Uncle Martin to his fate. But I could not allow him to be roasted to a crisp in his own house, though I shuddered with fear at returning to the scene of our horrible adventure. I was ashamed to admit this, so I held my peace.

'I don't know how you can still be sorry for that old scoundrel,' said Roddy with a sigh. 'We trusted him before, and you saw what he did to us.'

'Then perhaps we could tell the men that we have the money safe, and ask them to let him go free. They could send him into Galway and tell him to take the high road out of this part of the country....'

The very thought of this made the air around us seem sweeter. But Roddy said:

'I'm afraid that they won't agree to that now. We are not a peace-loving, forgiving people, Jim. I think the men are too angry now to let Martin Walsh go.'

'But if they get their money back. . . .' I said.

'It's hard to explain,' said Roddy. 'Taking their money was like taking a child out of every house in the parish. They never had money at all until a couple of years ago, and they thought they didn't care a hoot for it. But when it was stolen, it was easy to see that they thought it the most important thing in the world. It was not only for the money itself, you see, but that the money was the sign that they had succeeded. They are not mean, nor grasping. As well as that, they felt foolish for having trusted Martin Walsh, and they don't like to feel foolish. And another complaint is that they are behind-hand with the farm work and the fishing. They never waste a minute of the day, but they have wasted days and hours in the last few weeks at meetings and watchings, all on account of Martin Walsh. I'm afraid they are going to see that he pays for it.'

All this made sense to me. I accepted what he said there and then, and I gave up any ideas I might have had of leaving Uncle Martin to the mercy of the Cloghanmore men. I was content to thank my stars that I had Roddy on my side, to help me to save the poor sinner.

There was light in the kitchen window of Roddy's house, as we could see when we reached the foot of the boreen. On the curtains there were many shadows, of heads moving and bobbing and crossing to and fro. Roddy pulled up the horse.

'There's company in,' he whispered. 'I hoped we'd find my mother on her own.'

We did not want to march into the house, waving the bag and announcing to everyone where we had found it, at least until we knew who was present. I said that I would take the bag to the lean-to shed where I had rested against the donkey. I would wait there until Roddy could separate his mother from the rest of the people, and bring her outside. Then we would hand the money over to her, and our responsibility for it would be ended. Roddy agreed to this, but warned me that it might be some time before he would be able to follow me to the shed.

Along the boreen we got off the horse and turned him loose. 'When all this is finished I'll have a job to collect my property from all over the parish,' said Roddy. 'My cart and straddle below in Spartóg's field, my horse maybe wandered into Galway. . . .'

The horse whinnied indignantly.

'I'm very glad to hear it,' said Roddy. 'And you needn't play the innocent. It wouldn't be the first time I had to follow your hoof-prints over the half of Connacht.' He hit him a resounding wallop, and the horse galloped off into the darkness. Then he turned to me. 'Have you the bag safe, Jim?'

I assured him that I had. Silently we crept towards the house. At the gable we separated, and I went around by the back way to the shed. As I passed the back door I heard the crackle of women's voices in the kitchen. In the midst of them I thought I could distinguish the voice of Máire Spartóg, going like a threshing engine, without a pause.

The donkey was not in the shed. I went straight to the heap of hay, and felt it with my hands. The guns were gone. I leaned against the wall in a kind of daze, still grasping the bag, I thought that if it had contained a dead man's head I could not have loathed it more. It was the cause of all the anger and bitterness, I said to myself, and I wished I could have pitched it into the sea. But deep within me I knew that the real cause of the trouble was the mean soul of Uncle Martin. The bag fell from my hand, and I did not bother to pick it up.

I did not have long to wait, though the time passed like an age. Now that I had time to think of it, the knife-wound in my arm began to prick me. No sound from the house came through the thick walls, and it was only when Roddy was almost in the doorway of the shed that I heard his steps.

'Jim!' he whispered. 'Are you there? Jim!' There was an anxious note in his voice as he called my name for the second time. Suddenly he had lost faith in me. All at once I realised what a strange thing it was that he had trusted me at all. It

129

amused me to think that he was not so very much a grown man after all. No prudent man would have left my uncle's nephew alone with the bag full of money, which had been recovered with such difficulty.

'Here I am, Roddy, I thought you would never come back.'

I heard him give a quick little gasp of relief, as he stepped in beside me. Outside, I saw the shadow of Anna Faherty against the night sky. Then she too came into the shed. Suddenly I felt safe again. Her first concern was for me.

'Jim, you're hurt! Roddy told me that the foreign sailorman stuck a knife in you.'

'It's nothing,' I said. 'I haven't had time to think of it.'

'And you climbed the chimney, and found the money,' she went on in wonder. 'Aren't ye the two likely boys! Roddy, here, is as black as the ace of spades. He had all the women shrieking and praying when he put his head in the door. They thought he was the devil.'

It had never occurred to us that we must be covered with soot from both chimneys. I could imagine the scene when Roddy appeared in the doorway. I was glad I had not been there too.

'Every woman in the parish is in our kitchen this minute,' said Roddy, a trifle sourly. 'All the men are gone off to lay siege to the big house. They know your Uncle Martin is there. They think the foreigners are there too, and that they have got reinforcements from the sea. T e women say there will be murder done, and there they are, ologoning and moaning away like a pack of banshees.'

'Do you think that any more foreigners have landed?' Anna asked doubtfully. 'The men are so sure of it. They saw a strange boat.'

'I'll swear there was no one in the house when we were leaving it, but Uncle Martin alone,' I said. 'You could tell by the way he was running around and talking to the cat. Why would he bother to talk to the cat if there were people there to talk to?'

'Because he's cracked,' said Roddy bluntly.

'Roddy!' said his mother.

'Jim knows he's cracked,' said Roddy. 'If you heard the go on of him, and if you saw his nests and hidey-holes, you'd know well he's cracked. But I'd say Jim is right, for all that, and that there was no one in the house but himself. If there had been more sailors there, he would surely have brought them into the drawing-room and set them to watch while he climbed up and got down the bag out of the priest's room. He wouldn't have delayed. He's mad anxious to get away.'

'Anyway, the men think there is a small army in the house,' said Anna, 'and they're going to fight them to the last man. We all told them it wasn't worth it, but they have lost their tempers and nothing will stop them now.'

'Not even if they got back the money?' I suggested.

'Nothing will stop them,' said Anna. 'Anyway, we haven't time to tell them that we have the money. Show me that precious bag that's causing all the trouble.'

Roddy struck a light. Anna spread her skirts wide to shield the sight from the door. I opened the neck of the bag where it lay on the floor, and silently pulled up a handful of notes to show her. She gave a small cry, and then said very quietly:

'Close up that bag quick and we'll be getting on. I think I know what we can do.'

I tied the string at the mouth of the bag again. Then Anna took it and swung it high over her head until it rested on the rafters of the little shed. We packed hay around it so that it would not be seen, and then we started back towards the house.

At the door Anna paused.

'Leave the talking to me,' she said.

Then she flung the door open and we followed her inside.

Máire Spartóg had the floor, having, I suppose, silenced all the others by sheer weight of words. She was raising the keen, as we say, over Spartóg. One would think he was already dead, to listen to her.

'And my lovely Spartóg,' she wailed, 'who will go out now for me in the dark of the morning, and feed the pigs and the ducks and the little laying pullets? And who will milk the cow, and work the dash for me when my arm gets tired at the churning? And who will go lobster fishing in the proper season with all the men, and they singing the grand songs from boat to boat, and the grandest singer of them all will be gone! 'Twas my Spartóg was the king of them all, and 'twas I was the proud woman when he'd come home from the fair in Galway with the goldy pounds in the heel of his fist, and a present of delph, maybe, or a new shawl in a paper parcel for me. There's no one will ever bother to bring me a present now, Spartóg, with yourself gone and me getting old on my lone!'

And she started off on a long singing wail that sent shivers up and down my back.

'Hold your whisht, Máire!' said Anna sharply. 'You're wasting your keen. Spartóg is as hale as yourself.'

'But they'll take him in to Galway and they'll hang him on me.' She began the keen again, but stopped to add: 'And, anyway, how do you know but he's stretched below on the lawn of the big house this very minute, with a bullet through him, aye, and your own man, maybe, laid alongside him?'

She said that out of spite, I could see, because she hated to be stopped in the middle of her show. Anna took it in good part, however.

'Now you know very well the men haven't had time to reach the big house yet,' she said. 'And if you'll listen to me I'll tell you a great thing. The boys, here, have brought the money home!'

You can imagine what a sensation this caused. The kitchen was crammed full with women. There were big ones and small ones, young ones and old ones, fat ones and thin ones, fair ones and black ones. My eyes popped at the sight of them. There can have been no more than twenty of them, but in the little kitchen they looked numerous enough to fill our parish church. They were angry now, and I guessed it was at Máire

Spartóg, not only for her premature keen, but also because she had said that Spartóg was the best man in the parish. Now they were glad to be able to brush her aside. She looked very much put out, but she could not start up her wail again in the face of such an unsympathetic audience. Now all the women burst into cries of amazement, except Máire. She said, with large tolerance:

'Is it trying to make a fool of us you are, Anna?'

The chatter stopped and the others looked anxiously at Anna.

'I have the money in a safe place this minute,' she said soothingly. 'You know well I wouldn't deceive you,'

'That's right,' they said. 'She'd never make up a story on us and we so troubled.'

But Máire shook her head, and her strong voice rang through the room.

'All the same, I'd like to see it, and I'd like to know where it was found.' She turned on us with whirling petticoats. 'Would ye tell me now, young lads, how did ye lay hands on the money at all? Did ye find it out in a field, maybe, or stuck in a hole in the ground? Or maybe ye saw Martin Walsh himself, God between us and all harm, and got it off him?'

'We saw Martin Walsh, all right,' said Roddy, 'but he did not give us the money. We found it in Cloghanmore House.'

Still she wanted to see it, and it almost looked as if we would have to go out and bring in the bag and show her the contents before she would believe us. But Anna did not offer to do this. She appealed to the other women.

''Twould only be foolishness now to waste time showing you money,' she said. 'There isn't a woman here whose husband is not in danger. It seems to me that it would be a sin to waste time counting ha'pence when we should be down at Cloghanmore helping them.'

'I don't want to count it,' said Máire. 'I only want to see it.'

But the others suppressed her, and made her sit down and hold her tongue, a thing which I would have thought impossible. Then Anna went on:

'You know all the men are gone down to the big house ready for battle, with guns and knives and pikes and sleáns and every awful thing to kill the foreigners and Martin Walsh. Well, the boys say there's no one in the house but Martin Walsh alone. They have just come from there.'

'No one at all but Martin Walsh?' said a fair-haired woman who was sitting on the hob.

Roddy whispered into my ear that this was Peggy Scoot, Scoot Faherty's wife.

'Not a sinner,' said Anna. The women looked at each other with astonishment. 'So all we have to do is to get Martin Walsh out of the house, and the men can blaze away till they're tired, and no harm done. Roddy and Jim can get him out and away while we hold the men in talk.'

'But where will the boys bring him?' asked a very small but fierce-looking woman who was sitting on the table. 'Is he going to go scot free?'

'Yes, Mary is right,' said one or two others. 'We don't want him to get away free after all the heart-scalding he caused.'

'Then do you want your husbands to kill him?' Anna asked patiently. 'Because if you do, we can just wait here and start getting ready for the wake.'

But that did not please them either. At last Peggy Scoot said:

'We'll do whatever you say, Anna. You have more sense than the lot of us put together.'

'I don't know about that,' said Anna, 'but I'll do what I can anyway.'

While the women got their shawls from the back of the door, Roddy and I had a moment in which to wash some of the soot off our faces. Since we had come into the lighted kitchen, I had been trying to keep my eyes off Roddy, lest I might burst out laughing. I knew I was just as bad myself, but that was no help. He was a strange greyish-black, a colour that can only be achieved by contact with very old soot. His eyes rolling about reminded me of nothing more than of the white china eggs that we put under the hens to encourage them to lay. We did not have time to get off more than the outer layer of soot, but by the time we were ready to go we looked more or less like ordinary boys again. The taste of soap was far pleasanter than the taste of soot on our lips.

Just before we left the kitchen. Roddy reached in behind the flowery curtains and brought out a huge soda-loaf which had been set to cool on the window-sill.

'There's always one there at this time of the evening,' he said triumphantly.

I saw his mother open her eyes in astonishment as he broke the loaf and handed me one part. She looked a little more resigned when she saw how we fell on it, tearing off the succulent crust with our teeth and closing our eyes in bliss as we munched.

'God bless their appetites,' said all the women with respect, as they saw the death we were giving the loaf.

Outside the house in the dark yard Anna formed her little company into a double line. She said there was to be no talk for it would be better if the men did not hear us coming. She herself marched at the head of the army, with Roddy and myself at either side of her. Through scrappy clouds the moon looked down on us with amusement, and gave us just enough light to see our way. The women swung along as lightly as soldiers. I looked back once or twice and saw their wide skirts billowing out in the wind.

At the cross of the main road we met a man from another townland, riding home late and merry from Spiddal. He pulled up his horse sharply when he saw the procession of women. The moon shone out just then and showed every face white and determined in its hard light. The man on the horse blessed himself.

'It's the fairies!' he chattered. 'It's the fairies after capturing two lads!'

He began to moan and chatter that he would never drink anything stronger than buttermilk in future, and that he was a religious man, and that the fairies were not to touch him. All the time, the patient horse stood still in the middle of the road, blocking our path, and quite unconcerned at his master's foolishness. The women were delighted, and one of them gave a banshee wail for good measure. Another raised her voice to a cracked witch's shriek:

'It's Tommy Joyce from Lettermullen! Tommy, Tommy, will you come away with the fairies?'

It was Anna Faherty who put a stop to the fun. She gave the horse a thump that sent him thundering down the road with Tommy clinging to his back. Then we moved on, all the women in high good humour now.

I had never been to Cloghanmore House by the main avenue. I had always had to creep cautiously towards it from the direction of the sea-woods. Anna led us now to the main gate, and for the first time I walked by the proper way to my uncle's house. The avenue had obviously been long neglected. The trees arched thickly overhead and cut out the faint light that had served us until now. We stumbled over stones and fell into potholes throughout the length of it, so that we had to go slowly to save broken legs. Some distance away from the house the avenue forked. I could not see, but Anna said that the right-hand fork led around to the yard.

Where the main avenue had been stony and full of holes, the back avenue was a sea of mud. The women were very silent now. None of them uttered a complaint, though I was sure that their skirts must be caked with mud and slime.

'Thanks be to God, we have got here first,' said Anna presently, as we moved in among the trees. 'This gives you lads an extra bit of time. Off with you, now, while we wait here for the men.'

'But supposing they changed their plans and have gone to another place?' said Roddy. 'They could be attacking the house from a different quarter this minute.'

'I'll see to that,' she said. 'I'll scout around a bit and maybe meet them on their way. But I'm sure they won't change their plan, for they had it worked out very carefully.'

'Is it the old plan?' Roddy asked coldly.

'Yes, and I don't like it no more that you do. But I'd rather see twenty big houses burned than to have murder done. Now, off with you and get Martin Walsh out and away to safety as quick as you can.'

We arranged to bring him to one of the many sheep huts on the mountainside. Anna would visit us there next morning and bring us food. In a few days, she said, the men's tempers would have cooled off, and then she would talk them into letting him go.

11 Uncle Martin's treasure

A few minutes later, we were floundering up the muddy avenue to the back of the house. Until now, I had always thought that I liked the feel of mud between my bare toes. But this mud was cold and slimy, and it had a way of catching at you, almost like quicksand, that made our progress very slow.

As we neared the yard, the surface became a little more firm. Then, in the half-light, we saw that we were about to emerge on to the little path that led to the sea, beside the yard gate. It was clear that this back avenue was never used, for it ended in a path too narrow for any horse and cart. The accumulation of mud also showed years of neglect. Probably my uncle had always used the front avenue when he took his horse and trap in and out.

Roddy hurried on in front and waited impatiently at the yard gate for me to catch up with him. He had always associated with men, but I think he often found them too hard-hearted for his taste. Still I had no doubt that a few more years of struggling with the sea and the rocky land would harden his own heart too. Just now, it was easy to see that his mind was torn between loyalty to his father and pity for the poor old villain that we were trying to rescue. I was glad there was no time to discuss the rights and wrongs of the business.

'We won't go into the yard,' said Roddy. 'We'd be cut off there, once the gate would be closed. We'll go around to the front and look through some of the windows. And we're not going into any rooms this time. Once is enough to be caught out like that.'

'It would be better if we could keep out of the house altogether,' I said. 'If we could discover which room he's in we could talk to him through the window.'

Roddy agreed that this would be the best plan of all. Neither of us wanted to enter that house ever again. Indeed I had such a horror of it that I was almost glad it was to be burned down, secret room and passage and all.

As we reached the front of the house, the moon sailed out from behind the clouds and lit up the night around us. We wished it could have waited for another while. If the men of Cloghanmore were to come along now, they would be sure to see us. We could only hope that the army of women had managed to head them off, and were holding them in argument even for a few minutes.

There was a light in the drawing-room. The windows had been closed again, but the shutters had been left carelessly an inch or two open, so that we were able to see into the room. As silently as cats, we lifted ourselves up on our hands and almost pressed our noses to the glass.

Uncle Martin was there, all right. He was running about the room, as if he were dodging someone. He would run a few steps in one direction, and then change his mind and start off in another. Fursey wailed dismally around his feet, with his head thrown back. All he got for his sympathy was a vicious kick. Inside the hearth, a ladder was propped against the chimney wall. It was easy to see that Uncle Martin had been up there, and had found that his loot was gone.

Roddy rapped sharply on the window-pane with his knuckle. Uncle Martin stopped dead, with his head cocked on one side. Roddy rapped again, and this time the old man came scurrying over to the window, like a doll on wheels. He had to peer through the glass for a moment before he saw us. Then he started back in astonishment. I signalled to him to open the window. He flung it up, with an energy surprising in a man of his age, and stared at us blankly through the gap.

'Uncle Martin!' I whispered loudly. 'Can you hear me?'

'I can hear you, of course,' came his answer, in a dead small voice, apparently without interest.

But then his eye darted quickly from one to the other of us, like a snake, and I knew that he had not taken leave of his senses. I guessed that it was rage that had taken the life out of him.

'The men are going to burn down the house,' I said urgently. 'You must come away with us.'

'Why should I come with you?'

'We'll bring you to a safe place. The men will kill you if they find you here.'

'A safe place?' There was a queer mad note in his voice, without a doubt, like a violin gone out of tune. 'Was it you who took the money out of the chimney?'

'Yes, yes. We took it. It's safe now. You won't be able to get it back. Come on, for the love of goodness, or you'll be too late.'

'How did you find it? It was safe in the priest's hole.'

'There was a passageway from our chimney to the priest's hole,' said Roddy impatiently. 'Come on, now, Mr Walsh. Time is getting short. We must get a distance away from here before the men come.'

'How very polite you are,' he said exasperatingly. 'So they are going to burn my house. Yes.' We held our patience for a moment, and gave him time to think. Then he went on:

'And you boys have the money?'

'Yes, yes. Quite safe.'

Suddenly he lashed out savagely with his foot at Fursey, who had come purring and rubbing against his master. The cat danced away to safety, spitting viciously. Uncle Martin snarled, as if he had been another cat:

'And you let them get away with the bag, you useless, good-for-nothing bag-of-bones! I suppose you purred around them and encouraged them and maybe even opened the window for them –'

Roddy tapped his forehead for my benefit while he interrupted:

'Indeed and you're wronging the decent cat, Mr Walsh. He put up a great fight to save the bag; didn't he, Jim?'

'He did so,' said I with feeling. 'He sank his teeth in me.'

'Ay, and he called you there from the door, the creature, but you didn't hear him. Take him up under your arm now, sir, and we'll be going.' Roddy's patience broke at this point. 'For pity's sake would you grab that wretched animal and come along. Do you want to be found like a cooked sausage inside in the ruins of your house?'

'I'm coming, I'm coming,' said Uncle Martin testily. 'Don't be in such a hurry. There's plenty of time.'

But he seized Fursey unceremoniously by the middle and stuffed him under his coat where he held him tightly with his arm as a bagpiper holds the bellows of his pipes. Fursey made no attempt to scratch or bite, as he would have done with a stranger. A shiver ran down my spine as I remembered having heard that some people keep a cat in which is imprisoned an evil spirit who will work an occasional charm in exchange for a daily drink of his patron's blood. Uncle Martin certainly looked scraggy enough for the part, but I could not imagine him giving away a drop of blood in a lifetime, not to mind enough every day to feed a healthy cat.

The old man swung a quick leg over the window-sill. Sitting there astride, he took one long look back into the room. Then, without a word, he swung the other leg over and dropped on the ground between us. Over our heads the light still streamed out. I was glad that no one had thought of quenching it, because I hoped that it would arouse the curiosity of the men before they would embark on the burning of the house. I thought it possible that they would investigate, and desist from their project when they would find the house empty. This was the last thought that I gave the house. There was nothing at all that I could do now to save it.

We each grasped one of Uncle Martin's elbows, and trotted him briskly across to the path into the woods. We had decided

to travel along the shore first, because there was plenty of cover among the rocks. At the big valley we would take a boat and once among the canals we would be safe.

There is always something terrible about hurrying in the dark. We were no sooner in the wood than we heard the first sounds of the approach of the Cloghanmore men. It was a sort of murmur, of voices talking softly and of the rustle of undergrowth. They were bearing down on the house from the front. There was no mistake about it. We hurried forward, with an instinctive spirit of fear pricking at our heels. That these were our own people made no difference. At the clearing Roddy paused suddenly.

'Jim,' he said, 'we're surrounded. I can hear them coming into the wood ahead of us. Listen!'

I listened, and I heard the unmistakable sound of cautious boots on undergrowth.

'My mother wasn't able to head them off,' said Roddy in despair. 'What will we do with this poor wretch now?'

I realised that Uncle Martin was shaking with fright. He had shown no outward signs of fear until now, and I thought it was only the sound of our pursuers that made his peril a real thing to him. Between chattering teeth he muttered something. I bent my head close to him to hear. He said it again:

'The house in the tree.'

I repeated the words to Roddy.

'It's our only chance now,' I said. 'No one knows about it. We can hide there until the excitement is over. They'll never think of looking for us here, right by the big house.'

There was no need for me to argue the point. Roddy was already at the tree, and the rope ladder was sliding to the ground. In a moment we were hustling the old man up the ladder. He did not move quickly enough to please us, and we poked him on quite heartlessly. I remember that he gave little squeaks and grunts as he climbed, like a badger digging. Roddy followed on his heels. I came last and hauled up the ladder.

On the platform we paused to listen. The footsteps were coming closer. They were quite loud, as if the people saw no reason for moving quietly. I thought that they would start to go more cautiously when they would reach the edge of the wood.

'Inside,' Roddy whispered curtly.

Still keeping Uncle Martin between us, we crept into the little house. Then, while I held him, Roddy struck a light and lit the candle, which I still had in my pocket. He put it standing on the floor, where it was shaded by the box on which had been laid our dinner of duck. We had to have a light, he said, so that we could keep an eye on Uncle Martin.

'If it was dark, he could be scurrying around like the rat he is, and we none the wiser,' he said to me.

Uncle Martin looked at Roddy with hatred, but he said no word. It was clear that he regarded us as his captors, and certainly not as his rescuers. He could not forget about the money as easily as we had expected him to do. Boys are accustomed to putting failures behind them and starting afresh quite unconcerned. We did not know then what a bitter thing it is to a man to lose all the fruits of a careful plot. Now, as well as losing his loot and his reputation, Uncle Martin was about to lose his house. It was no wonder that he was not at ease, and I wished that Roddy had not insulted him.

With the mat in place over the doorway, we could no longer hear the footsteps outside. The house swayed gently in the wind. The creaking of the branches overhead and the high, light roar of the wind through the leaves, were the only sounds that reached us. Altogether it was rather like being in the cabin of a ship. I wondered how long we would have to stay here, and I was mighty glad of Roddy's presence of mind in taking the soda-bread. Otherwise we should have gone hungry, I thought, unless Uncle Martin had further stores laid in. This was not likely, for he had not intended to live here any more.

After five minutes that seemed like an age, Roddy said:

'I'm going out on the platform to see what's happening. Or

if I can't see I might hear something. No tricks, now!' he said sharply to Uncle Martin, who made no reply.

I was watching Uncle Martin, so that I did not see at once what happened next. The reason that I turned my head to look at the door was that I saw hope and triumph dawn on his face. I turned sharply. Roddy was crouched with his back to the wall and his knees bent, and an almost ridiculous expression of dismay on his face. In the doorway, smiling an evil smile, was the long-haired man. It was no dream. He was the same that we had left in Inishgower. While I watched, he stepped carefully into the room, bending his head for fear of striking it on the rafters. The little man slipped in behind him, and the mat fell back into place.

The big man saw the situation at once. We knew it by the slow contemptuous eye he turned on each of us in turn, and lastly on Uncle Martin. The little man darted straight across to me. I thought he was going to strike me, and I put up my hands to defend myself. But he made a grab at my belt, seized his own knife which was stuck in it still, and brandished it. I think he might have plunged it into my heart there and then, just to complete the drama, had not the big man called out to him sharply. Miguel dropped his arm reluctantly, and moved away a little, muttering. I was rather glad that I did not understand him.

Being within an inch of death is trying on the nerves. I sat down suddenly on the floor, and watched the business from that position for the next few minutes, while I recovered my wits. Presently I saw that Uncle Martin had perked up a great deal, and was twitting the big man with having been captured by us and landed on an island with only sheep for company.

'Did you drink sheep's milk, Pietro my friend?' he asked, and he laughed with mockery.

Pietro's brow darkened.

'If anyone ever mentions sheep's milk to me as long as I live, I'll slice him up in seventy pieces.'

'I thought it quite palatable stuff,' said Uncle Martin mildly.

'You heard what I said,' said Pietro between gritted teeth.

Miguel cowered, and looked as if he expected blood to flow at any moment. It was this that made Uncle Martin desist. Pietro went on:

'And it was you who were the cause of our capture,' he said angrily. 'Why did you not come back to the house this afternoon? You swore you would come back. We waited all day for you, risking our lives, and barricaded into the house like a beseiged army. And we risked a lot in sailing right in to Cloghanmore to get the *Saint Brendan* just to please you, because you could not bear to go without her. And now I see you have that old catto of yours under your coat, making more trouble. You know cattoes bring bad luck in boats.'

'Cats, not cattoes,' said Uncle Martin impatiently. 'And how could I go without the *Saint Brendan*? I've had her all my life. She was my father's boat, before I got her. She's not made of larch, like the other pookawns. She's solid teak.'

'I don't care what she is,' said Pietro angrily. 'We brought her to the slip and came up to the house, but you only came in for a few minutes and went away again. We thought you would be all ready to go as soon as we would arrive. All day there was no sign of you. Only this boy, peering in at the windows,' he jerked a contemptuous thumb at me, 'first at the front and then at the back of the house, until I hauled him in and made him talk. It is no wonder that I believed his cock-and-bull story. You had said that you would send me a message if you were not able to come yourself. I could see that the boy was a relation of yours. He is very like you in appearance.'

I stared at Uncle Martin with fascinated horror. Was it possible that I resembled him? I studied his miserable features, his wandering neck and his uncertain eyes. Did I look like that? I prayed that I did not. I knew that it was the spirit looking out of him that made him such an unpleasant sight. I resolved there and then to watch all my life for signs of my growing like Uncle Martin within, so that I should not look like him when I would be old. Pietro had noticed the effect of his remark on me.

'The boy does not seem flattered,' he said. Then he went on with the recital of his grievances. 'We have done all you asked us to do for our share of the money. You have kept none of the promises you made in your letters. Only that you had told us this morning about this nest in the tree, we might never have seen you again. Where is the good dinner you were going to give us before we set sail with the money? All we had was sheep's milk and wet potatoes on a desert island. And at the end of it all you have the gall to jeer at us, and laugh at us.'

I thought his fury would blow the house down. I was amazed at his command of English. But for a certain carefulness in his speech, and a very slight trace of accent, and that strange error about the cat, one would not have known that it was not his native language. If he was the sort of pirate that I took him to be, I guessed that he had an equal command of several other languages.

'I'm sorry I laughed at you,' said Uncle Martin pleadingly. He put a trembling hand to the side of his head. 'I am not well able to think. My head aches.'

'That makes me very sad,' said Pietro savagely.

Suddenly he asked the question I had been expecting.

'Where's the money now?'

'It's gone,' said Uncle Martin, and he began to cry like a baby, with big tears.

Pietro looked at him in exasperation. Neither Roddy nor I had said a word during the conversation between the partners. We were fascinated by the things that we were learning, and the more they argued and quarrelled the more we would hear of their association. But the main reason why we remained silent was that we wanted to keep the attention of the men off ourselves for as long as possible. It was clear that there was no question now of our taking Uncle Martin away up the mountains. It was we who were the prisoners now. With dull despair I wondered what was going to become of us.

Pietro was shaking Uncle Martin, and telling him to control himself.

'Where is the money gone?' he asked fiercely. 'Have you brought us all the way from Buenos Ayres for nothing?'

Miguel, scenting a job for himself, fingered his knife hopefully. Uncle Martin pointed a shaking finger at each of us in turn.

'Ask Jim where it is, and the other boy. They took it!'

Now we got plenty of attention, you may be sure. Pietro turned to us with a new interest.

'So you took it?' he said softly. 'When?'

'A small while ago,' Roddy stammered. 'A couple of hours ago.'

'Did Martin, here, give it to you?'

'No,' said Roddy. 'We found it ourselves.'

'And what did you do with it?' Pietro smiled in what he thought was a way that would inspire confidence. It reminded me of the way that a tiger might smile confidentially at his dinner. 'Now, think before you reply. If you can give me the money, perhaps I can let you go free, and Martin and ourselves can go away together quietly.'

And he showed his big white teeth again, in a grin.

'I can't give it to you,' said Roddy. 'My mother has it!'

Uncle Martin leaped to his feet. He threw himself across the floor, to attack Roddy. He had the face of an enraged weasel. Pietro caught him easily and held him. Uncle Martin twisted and struggled.

'Stop!' said Pietro. 'What a fool you are, my Martin! The Cloghanmore men have the money, but we have the boys!'

There was an ugly little silence. A smile of pure child-like pleasure overspread Miguel's face. He looked up to heaven and uttered a little pious exclamation of thanksgiving. Uncle Martin went slack in Pietro's hands, like a chicken whose neck has been wrung. Above his head Pietro smiled also, less sweetly than his servant. All three of them looked at us then, while we looked at each other.

Roddy's eyes darted to the door, and I knew that he was measuring our chances of making a run for it. Then he looked back at me, and shook his head.

'I should not advise it,' said Pietro. 'You would get no further than the platform.' He seated Uncle Martin on the box in the middle of the floor, as if he had been a child, and said: 'Now, Martin, we know that you can use your head when you please. Tell us what you think we should do next.'

Uncle Martin drew himself up a little, and a spark of life appeared in his dull eyes.

'The boys said that the Cloghanmore men are coming to burn down my house,' he said in a low voice. 'They were all about when we came here.'

'It's time you told me,' said Pietro contemptuously. He turned to Roddy. 'Is this true?'

'Yes,' said Roddy. 'We didn't want Mr Walsh to be burned, so we got him out of the house unknown to the men. We were taking him through the wood when we heard you in front of us. We thought you were more of the men, so we climbed up here to hide.'

With a quick movement, Pietro snuffed out the candle between his finger and thumb. Then he twitched aside the straw mat. Uncle Martin sprang to his feet with a little cry. We crowded in the doorway and stared, our differences forgotten. A red light shone behind the trees, filling the sky with radiance. Clouds of sparks went up in glorious bursts, like fireworks. A pungent smoke drifted towards us. Now we could hear excited shouts, above the roaring of the flames. The sea-wind sent huge tongues of fire high into the air. The house was well alight, for it must have been as dry as a St John's Eve bonfire. While we watched, flames looked out of the windows. Now the skeleton of the house stood out stark and black, outlined in flames. Uncle Martin gave a moan, and covered his eyes with his hands.

'We are too near that fire for safety,' said Pietro anxiously. 'A spark could set this old crow's nest on fire too, and there would be an end of us.'

'No, no!' said Uncle Martin wildly.

'What a coward he is, our bold captain,' said Pietro.

Uncle Martin had darted back into the middle of the room. In the glow through the open door, we saw him climb quickly on to the box. Then he was tearing at the soft thatch of the roof with both hands.

'He has gone mad,' said Pietro. 'He is pulling down the house around us!'

He thrust the end of the mat which he had been holding, into Miguel's hands, shouting to him to hold it high so that we should have light. Then he went across to Uncle Martin and tried to pull him down off the box. But Uncle Martin kicked at him savagely, so that Pietro staggered back across the room. He came forward again, but Uncle Martin was pulling away at the thatch, as if he hardly knew that his feet were engaged in fighting off an enemy. In another moment, perhaps, Miguel would have joined in the fight had not Pietro suddenly stepped back with a cry. Uncle Martin had found what he wanted. It was the first time that I had seen Pietro surprised. Off his guard, he was no longer the magnificent captain of the pirates. His face was the face of a poor greedy thief.

In his hands Uncle Martin held the biggest gold chalice I have ever seen. Precious stones glowed in the light of his burning house, and the gold shone like another little fire in our midst. Reverently he stooped and laid it on top of the box. Then he stretched upwards again and brought down a smaller chalice, and then a paten, all of jewelled gold. Pietro's sharp, quick breathing was the only sound in the little house. Roddy moved around until he stood beside me. No one tried to stop him.

There were nine vessels altogether. When he had taken down the last one, Uncle Martin climbed down off the box with a little sigh. He stroked the big chalice once with the forefinger of his right hand. Then he said dreamily:

'Now I'll put them in a bag, and we can be going.'

11 To the 'Cormorant'

Pietro swallowed twice, painfully, and then he looked at Uncle Martin with love.

'Where did you get those things?' he asked, in such a low, respectful tone that I wanted to laugh.

Uncle Martin answered him dreamily, like a man reciting a prayer.

'I have had them for a great many years. I was a young man when I found them first. They have been wife and child to me ever since. I never wanted to leave them. I never went away from my house without taking leave of them first. I have loved them and watched over them for twenty years. See how they gleam in the light. That's because I always kept them polished – '

'God save us from a curse!' said Roddy in my ear. 'Look at the miserly face of him! Look at the greedy paws of him! The devil has a hold of that man, for certain sure!'

Uncle Martin's hands were opening and shutting and rubbing each other, over the gold vessels, as if they had a life of their own. He certainly looked like a man that had an evil spirit in him, which now seemed to fill the little house to suffocation.

Again Pietro asked:

'Where did you find them?'

'In the priest's room,' said Uncle Martin, still in that faraway voice. 'But that does not matter. They belong to me. The priest is long dead.'

'You should have given them to the church,' said Roddy abruptly. 'Those are holy things.'

151

'Should I? Well, perhaps. But I prefer to keep them. They will bring me luck.'

'Luck! You miserable sinner! What luck have you had? I suppose it was for these you drove your own sister out of the house, as I've often heard, and let your house and land go to rack and ruin! And you may be sure it was they made a thief of you too, in the latter end, so that the hand of every man in Cloghanmore is against you.'

Uncle Martin smiled gently to himself.

'I'd do the same again to-morrow,' he said simply. 'They are worth it.'

'God bless my soul!' said Roddy, in horror.

Pietro had recovered himself by now. It was clear that he had done some quick thinking. Before Uncle Martin had produced his store of gold vessels from the roof, Pietro's only hope of profit had been to hold us to ransom for the money. He still intended to do this, as he explained now, but he had the comfort of knowing that even if he failed they would at least have the gold vessels, which would sell very well in Buenos Ayres.

Uncle Martin spread his hands over them.

'But they're mine,' he said querulously. 'They are not going to be sold.'

Pietro's eyes narrowed and he looked at Uncle Martin speculatively. Then he said cheerfully:

'Well, we'll talk about this later, if we get none of the money. You must pay your passage, you know.'

'Not with these,' said Uncle Martin stubbornly.

There was a short pause and then Pietro said:

'Well, well, let us not quarrel. Have you got a bag there, to put them in?'

Uncle Martin scrabbled in a corner and got out a canvas bag. If he had glanced at Pietro's face as he helped to pack the vessels into the bag, Uncle Martin would surely have seen that his ownership of them was at an end. One could almost feel how the big man was calculating the value of the stones and the weight of the gold.

As Uncle Martin tied the neck of the bag with a short piece of string, he looked up sideways and asked:

'How did you get away from Inishgower?'

'A boat passed close in, and we hailed it,' said Pietro. 'It was a man called Mattie Folano, sailing home from a christening. We told him our boat had drifted away, and he brought us aboard and sailed us right into your slip. He was a very nice man.'

Pietro went to peer out through the doorway, where the silent Miguel was still holding the mat obediently aside. The fire had settled down to a steady roar and the sparks flew up like spray. We could hear no shouting now. I wondered what the men were doing. I guessed that they would be overawed by now at what they had done, and would be seeking for ways to justify it. One thing was clear, that the showers of sparks were a real danger to us, and that we would do well to leave the house in the tree as quickly as possible. Pietro said to Uncle Martin:

'The *Cormorant* will be off Cloghanmore at midnight. I'd like to stay here until then, but it would not be safe. This place may go up in smoke at any moment. We must get down to the shore and wait there. One move out of you boys and Miguel will cut your throats – one, two! – like that! Now, quick move, please!'

We were hustled out on to the platform. Miguel's method of taking charge was to grip us painfully by the arms, with bony fingers. Pietro was the first to descend. We came next, with Miguel kicking at our fingers to encourage us to hurry. Next came Uncle Martin, hugging his bag of gold, with which he had refused to part. Miguel came last, and he moved in between us at once and resumed his task of armed guard. From the ground, the burning house was horribly near. The faces around me glowed strangely in its light. Roddy had turned his head away, and I could guess at a little of the sickness in his soul. I would have liked to have said a word of consolation to him, but I was afraid that he would not like it. In any case we were given no time for conversation. Pietro said sharply:

'Now, Martin! You know the way to that path down to the shore. Lead on!'

Uncle Martin trotted along awkwardly ahead of us, swaying a little from side to side like an aged sheepdog. He cut across the wood diagonally, taking us away from the direction of the fire. Presently I recognised the short, clean grass and the tall, moaning trees that I had passed through with the two pirates when I was taking them to Inishgower.

I began to think how Roddy and I might make a dash for freedom if we were able to give a signal to each other, or if it were just a little darker. We were effectively separated by Miguel's little body, so that communication was impossible. The red glow from the fire penetrated faintly even to this distant part of the wood. Our moving figures would show up too clearly as we flitted from tree to tree. All this I said to myself as we hurried along. I would not admit, even to myself, that we were too cold with fear to run. I think it was the sight of the burning house that had changed the whole adventure from a too exciting game to a terrifying cataract of events which seemed likely to end with our deaths.

The *Cormorant* was surely the same boat that the Cloghanmore men had seen earlier in the evening. And it was from this same boat that the two pirates had pulled ashore, before quietly casting off the *Saint Brendan* and sailing her around to the slip. I supposed that Uncle Martin commonly kept his hooker at Cloghanmore quay for safety from storms.

Now, all at once, I saw the answer to another question. I had not been able to imagine the *Saint Brendan* being towed by a bigger boat, all the way to South America. Neither could I see that the pirates would have a boat big enough, nor tackle strong enough, to take the hooker bodily on board. Now I remembered Pietro's narrow, calculating eyes, and the sidelong way that he had looked at Uncle Martin. I had often seen that same expression on a farmer's face as he reckoned up what day he would send a beast to the fair. It was a look devoid of love or interest, except in the value of the beast for sale.

Now I felt quite certain that Pietro had never intended to add a snivelling, good-for-nothing villain like Uncle Martin to his crew. He would never be fool enough to take him to South America, where Uncle Martin would be nothing but an embarrassment to him. Pietro had not risked landing at Cloghanmore quay to please Uncle Martin. He had gone there only because he needed the *Saint Brendan*. A few miles out to sea, Uncle Martin would be put into the hooker and cast adrift, to drown or to sail home as best he could. Pietro was not running any great risk in letting him go free. If the old man got home safely, he would not be very likely to complain of his treatment at the hands of the pirates. Ireland is not a good hunting-ground for pirates, and Pietro would lose nothing by never visiting it again. Other countries would probably offer richer pickings.

It was too much to hope that we would be cast off in the *Saint Brendan* with Uncle Martin. A pair of law-abiding boys loose in the world would be a daily threat to Pietro. He could not tell in how many years' time we might appear to accuse him of his crimes. Uncle Martin was old and weak and silly, but we were quite a different problem. Indeed it seemed to me that if Pietro were content to make off with the gold vessels, we were lost. Surely he would just take us out to sea and tip us overboard, and sail off quietly at peace with the world. It was quite possible that he would regard the entirely unexpected gold as compensation for the loss of the money.

While my brain worked furiously on all these problems, we had reached the path that led down to the shore. Uncle Martin did not wait for us, but trotted on between the tall rocks, and disappeared from view. Since we had to go in single file, Miguel went in front of us, and Pietro brought up the rear. We had not the faintest little hope of escape, sandwiched between those two desperadoes. Down between the rocks it was so black that we could not see beyond our noses. Overhead, the dark sky had a veil of pinkish smoke from the fire. All around us now we could hear the sound of the waves, strangely loud and fierce, as they often are at night. I felt as if all belonging to me had died.

In a moment we came out on to the shore. There was more light here, and it was easy to make out the shape of Uncle Martin, fidgetting from foot to foot while he waited for us. Now a roaring wind had added its voice to the din. The tide was in, and the white beach that I had seen earlier was almost covered with a twisting, tossing mass of dull black water. The moonlight touched it here and there, so that it seemed as if strange shiny monsters played in its ugly depths. I hated that sea, for I could feel that Pietro had already promised it my bones.

The big man whispered anxiously:

'There are the lights of the *Cormorant*. It's not yet midnight. I wish they would put off a boat now. They would if they knew that we are here.'

Away out on the heaving sea, I could see the riding lights of a small trawler, as I thought by their distance apart. Roddy turned to study them too, but neither of us said anything. I could almost have laughed at the way that Pietro had addressed his remarks to us, as if he expected us to sympathise with him in his hurry. Uncle Martin had become preoccupied with his thoughts, and was not heeding anyone. He clutched his precious bag to his stomach and rolled his eyes fiercely when Pietro touched him on the shoulder. I saw the whites shine.

'Well, Martin! We'll soon be safe!' said the big man heartily.

There was an uneasy undercurrent to his voice, though he had raised it and tried to sound cheerful. I could see that he was more concerned to keep up his own courage than Uncle Martin's. It reminded me of the way that the young men in my own place would whistle and sing passing a lonely graveyard on the way home from a late game of cards. By the way that my uncle jerked his shoulder away, I guessed that he was interested in nothing but his bag of gold vessels, and that he suspected everyone who came near him of wanting to lay hands on them. Miguel looked anxiously from one of them to the other, while he still held me and Roddy by the elbows.

I could see no sign of a dinghy coming towards us, though there could have been a dozen of them out there in the patchy darkness.

'If only we had the *Saint Brendan* now,' said Pietro impatiently, 'we could sail out to meet the *Cormorant*.'

A moment later, I'll swear he wished he had not spoken. Uncle Martin gave a short, sharp howl, like a shut-in dog that hears a fox in the yard.

'Quiet!' said Pietro in an angry whisper.

Uncle Martin howled again, with his nose pointing to the sky. Fursey, whom I had quite forgotten, poked his head out from under his master's coat, to see what was happening.

'My boat!' said Uncle Martin, in a sort of high whine. 'I won't stir an inch without my boat!'

I would have expected that Pietro would have flung himself on Uncle Martin there and then, and finished him off with his knife. I still do not know why he hesitated. It was not that he was squeamish about using his knife, as I well knew, by the practised ease with which he had laid it to my throat. It may have been that he was afraid that the sight of Uncle Martin's body would sting us into fighting for our freedom. Or perhaps he was not sure that his accomplices in the *Cormorant* would welcome a corpse in the dinghy on a rough sea. For I guessed that he would have had to bring the remains of Uncle Martin with him, lest they be found on the shore, and the hue and cry go out for his murderer over the whole world.

Whatever it was that stopped him, his hesitation gave Uncle Martin the start that he needed. He set off at a lumbering trot along the shore in the direction of Cloghanmore. He never once looked back, but clutched the bag to him fiercely and seemed quite unaware of the sensation he was causing. Pietro started after him. Then Miguel called out. Pietro turned back to answer. Miguel argued. Pietro answered fiercely. Roddy spoke for the first time since we had left the tree.

157

'A little bit more of this and Martin Walsh will be out of sight. What are they at, at all?'

I had guessed that they were arguing about us. Miguel had probably said that he would not be a match for the two of us, if he were left alone, and Pietro had answered that he was to bring us along too. Whatever the rights of it, a moment later we were being pushed stumblingly along the rocky shore after the disappearing figure of Uncle Martin.

The next part was like a desolate nightmare. One would have thought that a mile of ground separated us from the Cloghan-more men instead of a few hundred yards of a wood. We might have hoped every moment that someone would come walking along the shore, if we had not guessed that Anna had diverted the men in some other direction, to give us a chance of getting Uncle Martin away to the mountains. The men would have been excited and confused after the burning of the house, and she would have taken advantage of this to get them to obey her. It seemed that our plan had worked only too well.

At first I thought that Pietro would soon catch up on Uncle Martin and bring him back to the spot where the dinghy was expected to land. But Uncle Martin was on his own ground. He seemed to know every stone and every hollow along that coast. He skirted big grassy holes, while we fell into them. He hopped up and over rocks, while we barked our shins on them and fell sprawling. He ran along the top of the shore while we floundered in the pools below. All the time he kept a good twenty-five yards ahead of us. He was as agile and as wily as a middle-aged flea.

'We'll make a run for it at the quay,' Roddy gasped to me, in Irish, as we approached the village. 'I'm not going to be brought on to the *Saint Brendan* like an island cow going in to Galway fair.'

Miguel growled something at us his own language. I had no breath left for speech. In any case I did not think it would have been prudent to reply. I determined to watch Roddy, and to take a lead from him.

The village was lit up like day, when we saw it. It was close on midnight. On any other night the people would have been asleep by now. Tonight all the doors stood open, and lights streamed out from doors and windows. I could see people moving about. I did not know until afterwards that they were the old people and children who had been left at home to mind the houses. Down along the quay it was dark, with only a single light hanging high at the very end. A heavy, sloping breakwater was built out at the back of the pier. We would have to come up off the shore at the village street, in order to get around to the side where the boats were. I guessed that it was at that point, where the quay joined the street, that Roddy would try his break for freedom.

Uncle Martin was going a little more slowly now. The gap between himself and Pietro had shortened. I saw him glance over his shoulder once, his face shiny white in the moonlight. I could imagine what a strange sight he must be, with his cat and his bag of gold clutched to him. Except for the moment when he turned his head, he was only a moving shadow to me. Now Pietro was stalking him. Miguel hurried us forward. Uncle Martin climbed up the rolling shingle to the street, and slipped around the corner on to the quay. Two yards behind, Pietro followed him. Now it was our turn.

Just as we reached the street, Roddy kicked at Miguel's shins. Though Roddy wore no shoes, Miguel staggered back, surprised. At the same moment I was inspired to give a wild yell. For one moment we were free. But we had reckoned without Pietro. He was nearer than we had thought. Before we had time to tear off up the village street and in through one of the open doors he had taken three quick steps back to us and had us each by the collar. His fantastic giant's head with its long greasy hair and jangling ear-rings came down between us. The moonlight picked out his huge white teeth as he snarled:

'No more of that!'

Miguel, in a rage, was punching at us from behind. Between

159

them, they ran us down the quay so fast that we skipped every second flagstone. At the very end, under the light, they stopped suddenly. There below us was the *Saint Brendan*, her bows pointing out to sea. And sitting quietly in the stern, with his bag of gold vessels under one arm and Fursey under the other, was Uncle Martin. His face was turned up towards us, innocently waiting.

'Jump!' Pietro hissed into my ear.

I jumped, and so did Roddy, for we did not want to be thrown. Fursey spat fiercely. Uncle Martin did not move. Then Miguel jumped, and set the boat rocking. Pietro was working at the single rope that held us to a bollard on the quay. Just as he got it free, and threw it aboard, I looked back along the quay towards the village and saw the effect of the wild cry that I had given. I clutched at Roddy and pointed. Pietro was pushing off with the boat-hook, so that we were already a yard out from the quay. Miguel was hauling up the main-sail, dancing at the end of the rope like a little demon. A flurry of wind filled the sail. Pietro elbowed Uncle Martin aside to get at the helm. The hooker lifted on the swell. Only then did Pietro turn to look back.

Down along the quay the army of women was coming at the double. They were four deep. Their skirts ballooned all around them as they ran. It was easy to see the tall figure of Anna Faherty in the front rank. Roddy stood up in the boat and shouted to her. Now that we were out of reach, Pietro could smirk and heave-to so that the sail flapped. Then Anna's voice came clearly, echoing against the stone walls of the little harbour.

'Are you there, Roddy? And Jim?'

'Yes!' Roddy shouted. 'We're all here! Martin Walsh and his old cat, too!'

Now all the women were crowded along the quay wall, peering towards the boat.

'Ha, you brazen-faced thief!' came Maire Spartóg's voice. 'If you don't land them two boys this very minute we'll have the Guards after you!'

'You can have them any time you like,' said Pietro easily. 'Just throw me the bag of money here, into the boat, and I'll throw you the boys!'

'No, no!' Roddy shouted. 'Don't give it to them!'

'If you don't,' said Pietro, 'you will not see these valuable boys again.'

'We'll see about that!' said Roddy fiercely. 'It's not sheep you have!'

'Whisht, Roddy!' said Anna, and for the first time there was a note of fear in her voice.

Now we could see the women all huddled together, moving in and out almost as if they were dancing. It was obvious that they were consulting about what was to be done. After a minute or two they broke apart. Pietro, who had been sailing expertly around the little harbour, brought the boat around in a contemptuous curve and hove-to opposite where Anna was standing, a little apart from the other women. I thought how fine she looked there, in the light from the pier head, as proud and as straight as a ship's figurehead.

'You, there, big greasy fellow!' she called out. 'You must land the boys first and we'll bring you the money after.'

Pietro laughed indulgently.

'You are joking, Signora. It must be the other way about. You bring me the money, and then I will give you the boys.'

'We haven't got the money here. Surely you don't think we would bring it about with us?'

'I will wait for you,' said Pietro. 'I am a suspicious fellow, you see. It is part of my business.'

He was on top of the world just then. Helplessly we sat under Miguel's guard, and saw the big man raise his eyebrows triumphantly as the women put their heads together again.

'They'll go and get the money and hand it over,' said Roddy sadly. 'I know they must. Isn't it a poor thing to think that all our work was wasted, Jim.' He glanced at Uncle Martin. 'And this poor old gom, that thinks he's going to be brought safely

162

to South America, will be lying on the floor of the ocean before the night is out, himself and his scrawny old cat. . . .'

Until now, Uncle Martin had sat like a passenger, seeming to take no interest in our fate. Now he stood up slowly, squeezing his cat to him until it squealed. In a shaking, awful voice he said:

'What are you saying, boy? What are you saying?'

'I'm saying the truth,' said Roddy loudly. 'Do you think these heroes will be bothered to lose to your food, same, on the journey? Don't you know well that when they're finished with you they'll throw you away like the skin of an old potato!'

'Stop that!' Pietro snarled. 'Do you want to go the same way yourself?'

Suddenly the boat lurched over sideways as Uncle Martin made a wild lunge at Pietro. Taken by surprise, the big man let go his hold of the helm. The boom swung across, missing Miguel's head by a short inch. The hooker changed her course, and made straight for the quay wall, like a bolting horse. But at the last moment Pietro seized the helm and brought her around. Right under the startled faces of all the women we sailed. Máire Spartóg's open mouth and popping eyes oked ridiculous. Uncle Martin was weakly pummelling at Pietro, with little effect because he had only one hand free. The other still clutched the bag. He had dropped Fursey, who had retreated, spitting, to the roof of the little cabin. Pietro held the old man off easily with one hand, and managed to manoeuvre the boat with the other.

'After the little fellow, Jim! Get him down!' Roddy shouted.

We leaped on Miguel together and went crashing down on top of him, on to the bare ribs of the boat, all among the turf-dust and fish-scales. I got a mouthful of that mixture. The little man fought like a conger. Whatever part of him you grasped, he twitched it away from you at once. For a long, desperate moment, Roddy struggled for possession of his knife. Just when it seemed that Roddy had it, Miguel flicked it out of his hand. It flew through the air like a little rainbow and dived into the

163

sea. Miguel hardly seemed to notice. His feet worked like a donkey's hooves. He bit and scratched and jabbed and twisted. But there were two of us. We had him quiet at last. Panting, we sat one on either end of him, for one moment victorious. We looked down the length of the boat at Pietro, who had made no move to help his servant. I think we expected to see him shaking with fright.

He was leaning back easily, watching us, with an expression of amusement on his face. Uncle Martin was sitting slumped on the seat beside him, quite worn out from his part of the struggle. All at once I realised why it was that I could see all this so clearly. It was because we were sailing directly under the light at the end of the pier.

'Roddy!' I shouted. 'We're heading out to sea!'

Already we had rounded the high pier wall, and were leaving the light behind us. The *Saint Brendan* was climbing the long rolling waves, with that feeling for the open sea that all good hookers have. Now the moon sailed out into a clear patch of sky, and laid a wavering track on the hurrying dark water. We were on our way out to the *Cormorant*.

13 The chase

Now, too late, I saw that we ourselves had put an end to the bargaining for our lives. Pietro was no worse off for our having attacked Miguel. We could use him as a seat until we reached the *Cormorant*, if we wished, and no harm done. It took two of us to hold him down, leaving Pietro free to sail the boat. As for Uncle Martin, he was no danger to either side. He seemed almost to have forgotten his grievance against Pietro, or perhaps he had just become weary of the exercise of hammering at him. Whatever the reason, it was clear that it would be no use our looking to him for help.

Suddenly Miguel twisted away from under us. We sprawled on either side of where he had been. We had relaxed our hold on him for one moment, and he had been quick to seize the advantage.

'Let him go,' Roddy panted. 'Things can't be worse than they are.'

I saw Miguel crouch among the patches of light cast by the moon. I thought he would leap upon us again, but he did not. He seemed to have learned a little respect for our fists. Now, at a word from Pietro, he occupied himself with lighting the hooker's lantern, which he hung so that the light shone on the big man's face. This was an impudent gesture, I thought, and seemed to show that they no longer doubted their safety.

We retreated to the bows of the boat, where the little cabin was, and climbed on to its low roof. Here we sat with our legs dangling. There is something encouraging about even such a slight elevation. Looking back towards the dwindling lights of Cloghanmore, I found plan after useless plan coursing through my head. Roddy's soft voice in my ear might have been an echo of my thoughts:

'If we had six arms and six legs each, and if we could swim like whales, we might still get home alive.'

It was at that moment that I saw the other boats. I did not call out. I grasped Roddy's hand where it lay beside me on the deck. Even then, when I tried to speak, my breath nearly failed me. Then, in a low voice which I hoped would not betray my excitement, I said in Irish:

'Look back at the pier, Roddy. Do you see them too?'

For I thought they might be a vision sent to plague me.

Slowly he turned to look.

'I see them, right enough,' he said in the same casual tone. 'And it's not fishing they're going.'

Out from Cloghanmore they were coming, one after the other, as if it were the start of a regatta. We saw each one plainly for one moment only, as it sailed under the tall light at the pierhead. They slid out in a steady line, every big black sail full, and a gold line at the stern where the moonlight gilded the wake.

'They are all good new boats,' said Roddy quietly, 'and the *Saint Brendan* is old. But they are a long way off.'

'How many of them would you say there are?'

'About twelve, I think,' said Roddy. 'There's a few gone in to Galway with turf, and a few more went across to the Aran Islands for potatoes. But half that many would do us, if they can catch up on us.'

'This is a good boat too,' I said.

This was true. The *Saint Brendan* was clipping along at a great pace, sending spray up over us from her bows, dipping and rising so fast that she seemed to think she was on her way to America. Pietro was an expert sailor, and now that Miguel was free to help him, they were getting full value out of every puff of wind. If only that wind would fail, I thought. But there was no hope of that. There is nearly always enough wind, and to spare, off the coast of Connemara. Silent and undisturbed by our plight, the moon looked down on us. The hurrying black patches that were our only hope seemed very far behind. The lights of the *Cormorant* had become terribly clear. Now we could see the outline of her short, powerful hull.

'They'll never race us,' said Roddy. 'We've got too long a start on them.'

All at once I knew what to do.

'I'm going to climb the mast and cut the main halliard,' I said. 'If we don't delay this boat, we're lost. Just keep the little lad away from me until I'm out of reach.'

I had to borrow Roddy's clasp-knife, for I had none of my own. But he would not let me move yet. It was likely that we would have to fight the men away from the mast, and prevent them from mending the rope until the other hookers would have had time to catch up on us. That would have to be a short fight. It was painful to sit there and wait while every minute brought us nearer to the *Cormorant*.

But now we noticed that the boats were gaining on us a very little. Two had moved away from the others, and were tearing along side by side, as if they were racing each other. Though the rest were moving very fast too, they seemed to be plodding by comparison with the two leaders. We did not stare too hard at them, for we were still the only occupants of the *Saint Brendan* who had noticed them. Pietro and Miguel were watching the *Cormorant*, and they had not once turned back to look at Cloghanmore. I thought that they were watching for some kind of signa from their accomplices. We made a great show of looking fearfully at the *Cormorant* too, and I saw Pietro grin to himself in a satisfied way.

'I'll have a good laugh if it turns out to be our boat and Spartóg's out in front of the others,' said Roddy's voice softly in my ear.

'Why should that be?' I asked, glad to have something to talk about.

'When they were building the new boats,' said Roddy, 'everyone followed the old pattern exactly, except my father. He said that he wanted a faster boat, that would still be safe in a heavy sea. He worked out an improvement in the design, and started to build his boat. The other men used to come and watch us at work on it, and walk all round it and shake their heads. They said he was building a racing yacht, and not a fishing-boat nor a turf-boat. They said she would capsize in the first squall. They said there was one thing their grandfathers really knew, and that was how to build a boat. I nearly got to believe them myself in the end, and my heart was crossways the first time we went out in her. My father never had any doubts about her. He used to smile and say a word or two in her defence and that was all. He didn't try to persuade them to change their own plans. The only man who copied our boat was Spartóg. Máire Spartóg was wild. She lamented and wailed and said that Spartóg would be drowned and it would all be my father's doing. She came in and knelt on the kitchen floor in front of my mother and implored her to get my father to go back to the old design.'

'I can imagine her,' said I with feeling. 'What did your mother do?'

'She persuaded Máire that Spartóg was the cleverest man in the parish and that the other boats would all sink and Spartóg and ourselves be left floating. Máire went off quite pleased. She used to look very knowingly at all the other women who were so soon to be widows. They didn't know what was in her mind, of course, and I need hardly tell you that my mother didn't inform them.'

I looked longingly back at the boats and felt an aching hope that John Faherty's vision would yet save us.

At last Roddy judged that it was safe for me to move. About six hundred yards ahead of us was the *Cormorant*, strangely quiet, and showing no lights except from two lanterns hanging from the mast. The same distance behind us came the two hookers. The others stretched away beyond them in a straggling

line. I waited until the great black sail of the *Saint Brendan* swelled between us and our captors, and then I slipped quietly off the cabin roof.

When I was a very small boy, my great delight had always been to play among the boats that were tied up at our quay. This was why I had an accomplishment that was very useful to me now. Once I had spent many, many weeks learning how to climb a mast, gripping the wood between my knees and hauling myself up hand over hand until I hung from the very top. Now I stood against the cabin for a moment while I got the knife firmly between my teeth, to leave my hands free. Then I darted across to the mast. Roddy followed on my heels. I was up the mast like a monkey, faster than I had ever done it before. At the top I hung on with one hand while I sawed through the rope with the knife. The last strand twisted and turned away from me so that I thought I would never break it. When I succeeded, the effect was astonishing.

The huge weight of the sail pulled the rope through its pulley at once. The sail came down in a big wavering mass across the stern of the boat. The boom swung across amidships, dragging the sail with it. Then the boat heeled over. For a terrible age, I hung above the churning, heaving sea, waiting for the hooker to capsize. I was certain that we were all lost, for my weight clinging to the top of the mast tilted the boat over until the sea splashed aboard her. But then, very slowly, she righted herself. I could hardly believe that the mast was lifting into the air again, and that I was not to go down into those horrid depths whose jaws had been open to swallow me.

I got down off that mast a great deal faster than I had gone up. I leaned against it, panting, and looked about me. There was hardly any way on the boat now, with the sail down. She rode the sea quietly enough, as hookers usually do. I thought that even if she twisted and turned with the tide and the winds, she would not be likely to come to any harm from them.

A quick look back showed the two leading boats gaining on

us steadily. I could not know whether they had seen what had happened, but there was no time to signal to them.

In the stern, the falling sail had enveloped both Uncle Martin and Pietro. The lantern was untouched, and its light fell on the heaving, struggling mass of black canvas. I looked with distaste at Roddy's knife in my hands, and cast about for a weapon more to my liking. I found one at once, on the deck under my feet. It was a short, stout stick, with a handle whittled in it. I could not imagine what its use would be on a boat, unless it were to whack a recalcitrant fish on the nose. This was the use that I proposed to make of it now.

I seized it firmly and crept astern. The next time that a round bump appeared in the canvas, I drew back with all my might and brought down my stick with a mighty wallop. The bump subsided with a groan. Then, from somewhere behind me, Fursey sprang and clung to my back. I was wearing a heavy seaman's jersey, but his claws went through it easily. I whirled around, and smacked at him with my stick. It was impossible for me to dislodge him. He began to bite the back of my neck. I yelled to Roddy for help.

'Ha, you little tiger!' he panted, as he seized him roughly and pulled him off me.

I wished he had been more gentle, for Fursey took a mouthful of my neck with him. He tried to bite the hand off Roddy, but we got him into a lobster-pot, and left him to think of his sins.

When we turned around, there was Pietro crawling out from under the sail. His long, greasy hair swung around his bent head. He looked across the width of the boat at us, with his teeth bared, and naked murder in his eyes.

So it was Uncle Martin whose silly old head had received the blow from my stick. Chance had been against us there, for it might as easily have been Pietro. I remember marvelling at Fursey's devotion to his master, and the speed with which he had rushed to avenge him. Out of the tail of my eye, I saw Miguel climb on to the cabin roof, where he began to signal to the *Cormorant* with a flashlight. Roddy reached for his knife and took it out of my left hand.

'I hope we won't get close enough to be able to use it,' he panted. 'We must keep them off for a couple of minutes only, until the boats reach us.'

I turned sharply to look. I could hardly believe my eyes. I had been too busy to notice how much time had passed. The two leading boats were only fifty yards away. A great yell rose up in me, that might have come from a man three times my size. It started even myself, and Pietro started back as if he had seen a gorgon.

'Come on, you Cloghanmore men!' I roared, as if I had been at a regatta.

Roddy joined his voice with mine, and our combined noise was like to split the timbers of the *Saint Brendan* apart. I whirled my stick above my head like a drummer. I might almost have charged Pietro and demolished him there and then, if Roddy had not held me back.

'Dodge him,' he whispered. 'Wear him out. Keep him on the jump.'

A moment later, Pietro charged like a bull. His knife was raised high in his fist. He brought it down with force, where we had been a moment before. We fled up to the bows. Miguel was there, still standing on the cabin roof, signalling. We seized his legs and pulled him down with a crash into the bottom of the boat. Then we hopped up on to his perch and held our weapons at the ready.

Pietro, charging blindly, had fallen over Miguel, and the two of them were mixed up in a cursing, thrashing welter of arms and legs beneath us. Now the boats were less than twenty-five yards away. We could hear the people on them talking excitedly.

'There's women on those boats,' said Roddy.

''Tis only seagulls you heard,' I said.

Pietro was disentangling himself from Miguel, cuffing him around the ears and shouting at him.

'I'm sorry we came up here,' I said. 'If they come at us together, we're cornered.'

'As long as we stay on top we're all right,' said Roddy.

But he had forgotten that our main purpose had been to delay the boat. The instinct to save our skins had put everything else out of our heads. Now we saw that our two captors had recovered their tempers enough to see that they were wasting their time in chasing us about. Miguel was busily mending the cut rope, while Pietro stood guard over him so that no one should interfere. Now at last he had seen the pursuing hookers.

'Look at the big fellow's face!' said Roddy in an awed whisper. 'Anyone that tries to stop the little lad from mending that rope will be gone to glory in a brace of shakes. Just look at him! He'll stop at nothing now.'

'Will we attack him together?' I asked waveringly.

The very stance of Pietro filled me with terror.

'We'll wait,' said Roddy. 'It will take the two of them to right the sail.'

So we waited while the rope was mended. Every moment brought the hookers nearer. Then at last Pietro stooped to put his hand on the sail.

We were on his back like two stones from one catapult. We hung on to him as closely as Fursey had hung on to me, while Roddy jabbed with his knife and I whacked with my stick. We brought him to his knees. Then Miguel was upon us.

We were no match for the two of them. They punched us like boxers, and then they knocked our heads on the rail of the boat until we were quite silly. The boat rocked dangerously, which I think was the only reason why they stopped. Then Pietro panted:

'Over the side with them! That will give their friends something to do!'

But they were too late. Already one hooker was bumping against the side of the *Saint Brendan*, which became steadier at once. Then suddenly we were dropped, and lay there among the ropes and lobster-pots unable to move. The next thing I knew was that Máire Spartóg was standing over us, giving out a long speech. I only heard a part of it.

'Wisha and there ye are, my two haroes, with the life nearly battered out of ye by those great thieving ruffians! Ye're safe as a pet cat now, and the two boyoes are below and they spancelled together like two old goats that would be wandering the roads. I'm telling you they'll catch it when the Guards get them! And you'll be above in Máire Spartóg's kitchen and you guzzling the potful of white cabbage, and the lovely sweet red bacon, and the bursting-laughing potatoes, and telling the company the great doings ye were at. Oh, there's good times coming, so there is, and only for Spartóg being the clever man to build the good boat, you'd be gone down this minute into the salt sea, and it's raising the keen over you we'd be instead of breaking our hearts laughing.'

'Faith and it's yourself is well able to lament and wail,' said John Faherty's voice behind her. 'I hear you had us all dead and buried a while back, above in the house.'

'Arrah, go on, now, John,' said Máire good humouredly, but she moved away from us all the same.

Then Roddy's father was bending over him, asking anxiously if either of us were hurt, telling us that it was true that the pirates were tied up and that we were all ready now to sail home.

'And Uncle Martin?' I asked weakly.

'There's not much fight in him now,' said John pityingly. 'He has got a crack on the head, anyway, that would keep him quiet even if he were inclined to be wicked.'

'I did that myself,' I said, 'but it was meant for Pietro.'

'It was a good crack,' said John delicately.

Presently we sat up and looked around us. My head spun with pain, but I cared nothing for that now. The sea was alive with hookers. Roddy had been right about the women's voices. I could hear them all around me now from every boat, like the soft voices of swallows. They say that women bring bad luck in boats, but this time it had been the other way about.

We were helped out of the *Saint Brendan* into John's boat as if we had been invalids. Anna was there, with a billy of tea waiting. As I drank it, I could feel the terrible excitement die down in me. In the stern, when I turned, I could see the two sullen pirates, helpless now in their bonds. Uncle Martin was there too, with his head sunk on his chest.

14   The end of the story

There was still no sign of life on the *Cormorant*. There she rode, a little distance away, her two lanterns alight, like a liner at anchor. I could not understand it. While I stared at the little ship, Roddy left his mother and came to kneel beside me. Then we saw two hookers slip away from the others and make towards her.

'That is Scoot's boat,' said Roddy, peering into the darkness.

He could not say who owned the other boat. We saw them sail right up to the *Cormorant* and melt against her. We waited for a while, until presently one of the hookers came ploughing back towards us. It was Michael Mór Nee's boat. He hove-to and gripped the side of our boat to shout above the noise of the wind:

'There isn't a sinner on board that boat!'

The other boats drew near and clung to another. We were like a big raft going up and down on the swell in unison.

'How can that be?' said John Faherty in astonishment. 'Sure, someone must have sailed her in. She has been in and out all day, but she wasn't there at the fall of night.'

'She was not,' said all the men emphatically.

Pietro lifted his huge head.

'She came in to take us away,' he said contemptuously. 'I can believe that my men were stupid enough to leave her.'

He shut his mouth suddenly, as if he had realised that he had said too much. John looked at him for a moment before he said softly:

'I'd swear my oath the crew of that trawler is gone in to the slip in the dinghy.' Pietro turned away his head. 'So that's it. Well, we can pick them up at the slip later on. What class of a cargo is on that boat, Michael Mór?'

'Man, 'twould take the sight out of your eyes,' said Michael Mór. 'They must have robbed a king, at the very least. There's silver things and gold things, and bales of cloth with pictures of big flowers and parrots on them.'

Pietro made a little wailing sound.

'I do business with dealers in Europe,' he said sharply. 'Your friend makes it sound like I am a thief.'

'He does, faith,' said John solemnly, and the men burst into a gale of laughter.

Now at last we started for home. Some of the men stayed behind to bring the *Cormorant* in to the quay. They were very much excited at the thought of owning her, and they quarrelled like children about who should ride in her.

Spartóg got into the *Saint Brendan* and we took her in tow. Uncle Martin showed his first sign of interest when he saw that we were going to look after his beloved boat. Spartóg's own boat was brought in by his son, Ned. They only other passenger on the *Saint Brendan* was Fursey, who had managed to crawl out of the lobster-pot. He sat beside Spartóg all the way home. Spartóg did not like his company in the least. He tried to smack him away with his hand, and called him a criminal cat, but Fursey would not move.

With the weight of the *Saint Brendan* to hold us back, we were soon left behind by the rest of the fleet. They slid past us one by one, hurrying home towards the light on the pier-head and the lighted houses. Presently, away off in the darkness ahead of us, we heard one of the men start up a song in Irish. The other men in his boat joined in and they sang the first verse. Another boat took up the next verse, and so it went on from boat to boat. Between the verses they all sang the chorus. I could not hear the words, for the voices became fainter as they

177

drew farther and farther away from us. But I knew the song well. It was a song about a fisherman who caught a mermaid in his nets. The chorus said that many strange and wonderful things are brought in from the sea, hóró, hórá!

'The people in the village will hear the singing,' said John, at the helm. 'They will come running down to the quay to welcome us. Thanks and glory be to God that this night's work has ended so well!'

'If you had not been after us in the boats so quick, it would have had a very different ending,' said Roddy. 'Why did you come back to Cloghanmore so soon?'

'We thought you would be busy burning down Uncle Martin's house for the next few hours,' said I.

'Ah, that was a bad business, a bad business.'

'I always told you that it was,' said Roddy quietly.

'And you were right. 'Tis a terrible thing when a grown man has to learn sense from his son.'

'Often you told me you were able to teach sense to your own father,' said Roddy solemnly.

'Tell us about the fire,' I said quickly.

Anna had heard every word, I knew, though one would not have thought it. She stood in the bows, quite straight and still, with her back to us. Once I thought she was going to turn around, but she just gathered in her shawl about her as if she were cold, though she lifted her face to the night wind.

'I'm heart sorry about your house, Martin,' said John sincerely. Uncle Martin made an impatient movement, but he said nothing. John went on after a moment: 'By the time we reached the big house we were all in a raging temper. We had spent the whole day, nearly, talking over in the shop, and the more we talked the crosser we got. We marched along in a body, carrying our guns and cans of lamp-oil, shouting and roaring about revenge – oh, a disgrace to the world! I was the worst of them myself, I will admit. We quietened down when we reached the gate and we came up the avenue, and surrounded the house.'

'Jim and myself heard you,' said Roddy. 'We had just slipped Mr Walsh, here, out of the house in time.'

'The next thing was that your mother and all the other women were all around us, telling us to come home quietly and not be disgracing ourselves, telling us they had the money safe and that Martin Walsh had left the house. We were that mad we wouldn't even listen to them. We brushed them away. We said this was men's business. We said they should be at home darning our socks.

'We broke down the front door and rushed into the house. We poured oil on the stairs and along the passageway above. Then we opened all the windows and doors. We kept shouting to Martin to come out. We thought he must be hiding somewhere in the house, when we found the front door barricaded.'

'We had got him out of the window,' said Roddy.

'I had a sod of turf ready,' John went on, 'with one end of it soaked in oil. I lit it and threw it in through the open door. A moment after I had thrown it, I wished I hadn't. But it was no use by then. The stairs caught fire first, and then the fire ran along the little trail of oil that we had laid up the stairs. It was a fine dry old house, and with the wind that was blowing, in ten minutes it was blazing like the fires of hell.'

'We saw it, from the house in the tree,' I said, very quietly.

'The fun went out of it all suddenly,' John went on after a moment's pause. 'The men began to gather around me. We all stood there looking at the blaze. The women were in a little group by themselves, looking at us. We couldn't say a word. I began to understand what they had told us. I went across to Anna. I could see her plain in the light from the fire.' Now he seemed to be talking to himself. 'There were tears in her eyes. I never saw her like that before, not even when the cow died. "Anna," I said, very soft, "did you say that you have the money of the Cloghanmore men?" "I have it," she said. "I have it safe at home." "And did you say that Martin Walsh is gone out of the house?" "I said that," says she.

179

'It was your mother that told us to come back to Cloghanmore. She said there was nothing we could do to save the house now. She said the woods were so wet from the rain that there was no fear of them. We would have done anything in the world that she told us, just then.

'All the women went out in front, and we walked after them, quiet and sober. There wasn't a man there could look another in the face, though we had only done what we had come out to do. The one thing that pleased me was that Martin Walsh was not in the house, to come running out like a rabbit out of a burrow. We had our guns, and who knows but one of our men would have shot him down. That would have been a terrible thing. Oh, Roddy don't ever get so cross that you have no hold on yourself. 'Tis like a madness.'

'I'll remember that,' said Roddy gently.

'So we came along as far as the quay. We were a little way behind the women, because we didn't want to walk with them, and because we had stopped to leave our guns in Paddy Conneeley's shop. All at once we heard the shout. 'Twas one of you boys.

'We saw all the women run down the quay. We followed them, not very close. We arrived just in time to see the *Saint Brendan* heading out to sea. At any other time we'd let no women into the boats, but this time they didn't ask us. Every man found his wife and his sisters and his aunts and nieces there in the boat waiting for him. Ne'er a one dared tell them to go ashore.

'We thought we'd never reach you in time. We heard shouting, and fighting, and we saw the sail come down.'

Anna turned suddenly and said:

'Only that your father was clever enough to build the good boat, we'd be going home to your wake.'

We were silent then for a while, until Uncle Martin edged nearer to me and said:

'I'm not sorry after the old house, Jim.'

'Then I don't see why I should be,' said I shortly, for I was sore and hurt at its end.

Anna came and sat at the other side of him.

'What came over you at all, Martin?' she asked, as if there were no one there but the two of them. 'You were always a sparing kind of a man, but you never did anyone wrong. How did you take up with those two bad ha'pence there? You should have known they would be your ruin.'

He did not answer for a few minutes. She put out her hand and laid it on his sleeve. Then he spoke, in a light, dead voice, as if he were talking of faraway things, or as if he were on the edge of tears.

'It all began with the gold vessels. Anna. Yes, that was the beginning of it, nearly twenty years ago. My old cat climbed up the drawing room-chimney, and he didn't come down again. That was long before Fursey, of course. I wondered where he had gone. My sister, Mary, was there then, Jim's mother as she was afterwards. I waited until she had gone to Cloghanmore with the butter – she was a grand butter-maker. We had twenty-one cows that time, if you count the beast I had bought at Galway fair the week before. That was the last beast I ever bought.'

'What did you do when Mary was gone with the butter?' Anna encouraged him, as he fell into a brooding silence.

'What's that? Oh, yes, I was afraid that she would laugh at me for bothering about the cat. The cat had gone up the chimney, Anna, and he hadn't come down, I was worried about him.'

'Yes, Martin. You were telling me about him,' said Anna gently.

'I told the little girl we had working in the house to go and bring home the cows,' said Uncle Martin. 'Then I got the ladder, and put it in the fireplace, and climbed up to look for the cat.'

'And what did you find in the chimney?' she asked eagerly.

'Don't hurry me,' said he petulantly.

We drew back a little. We had all been hunched forward to listen, except John, who tended the helm like a man in a dream.

181

The black gleaming water hurried past us, white and gold in the glitter of the moon. I could hear the boat's timbers creak as she climbed the long waves. I would gladly have shaken Uncle Martin then, if I had thought that I could have shaken the rest of his story out of him. He went on in a moment, with a sort of rush:

'I found a little dusty room in the chimney. It was lightsome enough, from the big open fireplace. The cat was sitting there, waiting for me. I found the old gold vessels all set out in a row at the back of the room. I didn't know that they were gold at first. They were dull, and covered with tarnish and dust. But I got a cloth, and I put paraffin oil on it, and I cleaned them off. Oh, they shone like little lamps then, and I loved them, every one.

'The next day, I told the little working-girl to go home to her mother, that I had no more money to pay her. Then I used to watch my chance until Mary would go out. She was a hard-working girl, a lot younger than me, and she was only wanting to please me. But what would have pleased me most, if she had known it, would have been for her to go gallivanting over to Cloghanmore to the dances, and for a gossip in the shop, the way I could go up to my little room in the chimney and handle my lovely gold cups and count the jewels in their eyes.

'At last I made up my mind that I must get rid of her altogether. We had a man working the land, a man called O'Malley from Borris. My sister was friendly with him, but I didn't ever fancy him myself. I thought it would be a good idea to have the pair of them out of the way. I told her she'd have to marry him.'

Anna gave a little gasp at this. Then she smothered the sound quickly in her shawl. John and Roddy were quite motionless. I clenched my fists, lest my hands might reach out of themselves and twist Uncle Martin's scraggy neck. He was going on with his story, with no idea of the venom that he had aroused in me.

'Mary didn't like that. I said to her: "You're forever telling me what a fine clever fellow John O'Malley is, and how he has a farm of his own at home, that he can walk into any day. Well, what is to stop yourself from walking into it with him? You'll have to get married some time, and you might never do better." 'Twas a hard way to talk to the girl, as I can see now, but I was that mad to be left alone with my gold. She said it wasn't decent. She said she'd be shamed. She said the neighbours would say that we were a terrible family. While I was arguing with her, John O'Malley came into the room behind me. He heard me telling her to offer to marry him, that he would be delighted to get her. That's one man I can never like. He came loping across the kitchen floor and laid me out with a blow of his fist.

'When I came to, I was still lying there on the cold kitchen floor. They were gone, and hair nor hide I haven't seen of the pair of them ever since. After a while, Mary wrote to say that she was married to John O'Malley, and that they had a nice place and were very fond of each other. Oh, she was a good, forgiving sort of a girl. Then afterwards I heard that there were some children. I didn't ever write to her but the once. I was too busy.'

Again there was a long pause. Anna had drawn away from him again. We were coming close to the pier now, and I could see dark figures about like bees at the hive. I wondered if Uncle Martin would have time to finish his story before we would have reached the quay. At last he went on:

'I did no more farming after Mary and gone. I sold the cows, because I couldn't be bothered milking them. I had some money in the bank in Galway, that my father had left. I used that to buy food. I didn't need much, because I found that I didn't get hungry any more. I chased away anyone that came to the house, and I frightened the little boys that used to come to play in the woods. I wanted to be free to go up to my little room whenever I liked.'

'Oh, the long wasted years!' Anna burst out.

'It was lonesome then,' said Uncle Martin, as if she had not spoken at all. 'I had never thought of that. I think I lost track

183

of time after a while. The priest came to see me many times, but I used to shut myself up whenever I would see him coming. At last he did not come any more, and I was glad. I knew that if he saw my gold vessels, he would take them away to his church.'

No one made any comment on this.

'Every second Wednesday I used to go in to Galway to draw out my little bit of money from the bank. One day when I was in the shop in Cloghanmore, Paddy Conneeley asked me if I would bring in some money belonging to the men of the parish, every time I would be going. I agreed to do this. I used to call into the shop and collect a little bag of money, and take it into the bank, and bring home the receipt. At first I wasn't much interested. Then bit by bit I began to notice that the sum of money in the bank was growing.

'One day, about a year it would be, while I was in the shop, Pietro and Miguel came in. I was handing the receipt for the money to Paddy Conneeley. I took no notice of them. We often have foreign sailormen hereabouts.'

'Paddy remembers that day very well,' said Anna.

At the mention of their names, the two pirates had lifted their heads. They watched Uncle Martin's face steadily during the rest of his story.

'When I came out of the shop, there they were waiting for me. They walked home with me, one on either side of me. I liked that. No one ever came to see me. I was getting lonely.' He dragged out the word, to make us feel sorry for him. No one said anything. He went on after a moment. 'I told them about the money that I brought to the bank every fortnight. They said nothing about it then. They talked a lot about their travels, and about the warm, sunny countries that they knew. I thought of our shivering winter here, and I envied them.

'When they had gone, I began to think for the first time of leaving Cloghanmore. I did not do anything. I had not much money. I never thought of selling my gold vessels, no more than a man would think of selling his wife, or his child.

184

'A few weeks later, Pietro and Miguel came again. They landed at the slip this time in a dinghy. They brought food with them, and bottles of wine. We had a feast in the kitchen. We had a strange big pie that they called a *pizza*, full of tomatoes and a kind of cheese like elastic. They heated it at the fire. I had not eaten so much for years. That and the wine made me very brave. They said that I was wasted in Cloghanmore. They said that I had the bold spirit of a gentleman of fortune, and they asked me to come away with them.'

'Mama mia!' Pietro burst out fervently at this point.

Uncle Martin turned and shrieked at him.

'You did, you tempter! Every few weeks you were in through my kitchen door, with your talk of easy money and a new life. You got out a piece of paper and you added up a long sum, the amount of the Cloghanmore men's money.'

'Who told me the figures to put down?' said Pietro contemptuously. 'Who worked out the plan for getting the money out of the bank? Who built the house in the tree and went into hiding there? Who made a fool of us in the end and tried to cheat us of our share of the gold cups?'

'I am a wicked old man,' said Uncle Martin simply. He reflected on this for a moment and then went on: 'Yes, I did all those things. I drew out the money. I was to go away to South America with Pietro. He was to have one-third of the money for his trouble. I was foolish to believe that he would be satisfied with that. I thought he would leave me my share and land me safe in Buenos Ayres.'

'You would not have come outside Galway Bay,' said Pietro through clenched teeth.

'In the end I was getting frightened of the two of them.' Uncle Martin was jabbering now in his excitement. 'I was afraid of them. I was very pleased to see Jim. I thought he would help his old uncle. I sent him down to watch what the men were at, but they saw him and he ran away. I had brought my gold vessels to the house in the tree, but the money was still in the

185

secret room. I was afraid that Pietro would find it. I thought he
would sail away without me. I would not have let him get it
that way, I would rather have given back the money to the Cloghanmore men. 'Tis hard to do right by everyone.'

We were all silent at this.

'Ah, yes,' he sighed, 'it's good to be on my way back to my
own village again, safe and sound, with those two tempters tied
up where they can do no more harm.'

'We must send the gold vessels to the bishop, Martin,' said
John quietly.

I thought he would begin to shriek and cry at that, but he
said, quite calmly, after a moment:

'Yes, that would be best. I don't want them any more. They
deceived me.'

One would have thought he was talking about fellow men.
Pietro made no remark at all. He fixed his eyes on John Faherty
with a sort of angry dignity that I found very disturbing.

When we reached the quay, the other boats were already tied
up. They had left a space for us, and we slid in easily, guided by
many willing hands on our gunwales. The whole village had
come down to the quay to welcome us. All the grandmothers
were there, carrying the babies in their shawls. The children
ran in and out between their legs. The bolder ones came over to
stare at the pirates in astonishment. The old men were speechless with delight and pride.

At last we were walking up the quay to Paddy Conneeley's
shop. His mother greeted us at the door. She was a tiny woman,
eighty-six years old, but she had not been idle while the men
and the younger women had gone to our rescue. She had prepared a feast fit for a victorious army, in the huge kitchen behind the shop.

'How did you know we would be celebrating?' Máire Spartóg
asked her jealously. 'How did you know but it would be two
corpses we'd be bringing back with us?'

'Wouldn't the feast have done for the wake?' retorted Mrs

Conneeley, with that grand lack of concern for death that is often to be seen in the aged.

Even Máire was silenced by that.

After supper, the story had to be told and retold for the remainder of the night. Everyone's questions had to be answered. Then Uncle Martin's bag of gold vessels was opened up, and the contents passed from hand to hand for inspection. They all agreed that they must be sent to the bishop in the morning, for he was the person who would best know what should be done with them.

No one mentioned the burning of the house. I guessed that that would be a forbidden subject in Cloghanmore in future times. The women made skilful use of their husbands' guilty feelings, and also of the fact that it was they who had manned the boats and hurried the men down to the quay to our rescue. At first the men could not believe that their wives wanted to let the pirates go free.

'But they are criminals!' Spartóg spluttered.

'So are you,' said Anna calmly.

'But they stole our money, they abducted Roddy and Jim –'

'They didn't get away with either,' said Anna, 'and the worst day they ever were, they never burned a house.'

The pirates had been listening to all this. They had been brought in, under strong guard still, and had been given food by the women. The men had tolerated this, for they had been sure of having the satisfaction of seeing them marched off to gaol in the morning. It was quite comic now, to see how John and Spartóg and Scoot and the rest of them resented the way in which Pietro began to perk up again, at the prospect of freedom.

'How do we know they won't come back again and make another try for the money?' said Scoot weakly.

'They won't come back,' said Anna confidently.

'That is quite certain,' said Pietro with feeling.

After more than an hour of argument, the women had their way. When the Cloghanmore men found that they would have to give up the *Cormorant* too, it almost looked as if they would never agree. But at last, as dawn was breaking, we all went down to the quay in a body, and put the two pirates aboard their ship. Uncle Martin came too, with Fursey under his coat. The crew of the ship, four dark-skinned fellows without a word of English or Irish between them, had been found with their dinghy at the point below Cloghanmore House, where they were to have picked up the captain and his servant. Pietro looked as if he would beat them later on, for having left no one on the *Cormorant* when they took the dinghy ashore. As we watched the little ship move away from the quay, Spartóg said sorrowfully:

'It's a sin and a shame to let all the fine cargo go away again so quiet.'

'Maybe you'd like to be a pirate yourself, Spartóg, in the end of your days,' said Máire sweetly. 'Maybe you'd plough the Spanish Main and bring me home a sack of gold, like the lad in the song.'

Spartóg growled, but he said no more.

I settled down in Cloghanmore. Paddy Conneeley's mother took Uncle Martin into her little house in the village, and said she would look after him. He became very religious, and took to spending a lot of time in the church, pattering off prayers at a great rate. Perhaps the blow on the head that I had given him had done him good. Gradually the village people became quite respectful to him. I even heard one man say that he was a saint, but that man was soft in the head.

Uncle Martin and I became very friendly. I farmed his land for him, which he had not done for so many years. It was some of the best land in that poor place. I made it pay, and it was this more than anything else that made him so fond of me. He never lost his miserly habits, and he never lifted a hand to help me at the work. He used to stand in the field and watch me plant the potatoes, or sow the corn, and chat away to me about old times in the barony. He seemed almost to have forgotten his former wickedness.

He never went back to the house in the tree, so far as I know. This was a good thing. It had almost been wrecked in the scuffle just before we left it, and he would have been cruelly disappointed.

Roddy and I went there often, and did what we could to repair it. I stayed with John Faherty and Anna, where there was plenty of work for me to do. The seaweed factory was built at Cloghanmore, and brought great prosperity to the district. While it was building, Uncle Martin used to go out every day to watch its growth. At last the workmen held a meeting, at which they made him Honorary Foreman. He was delighted with this, and he assumed an air of ownership which gave the village people a great deal of amusement.

He made me a present of the ruins of Cloghanmore House. I thought of rebuilding it, but my mother would not agree to this. She said it had brought misfortune on her family, and she could not regret that it had been burned down. I did not go against her wishes.

The Lost Island

The lost island of Inishmanann drew Michael's father away in pursuit of a legend, and four years later he has not returned. After receiving a message through an old tramp, Michael sets sail with two friends, hoping to solve the mystery and bring his father home. However, other people are interested in the island too, and the dangers of wind and weather are not the only ones the boys have to face.

Eilís Dillon is the author of numerous children's books and *The Lost Island* is one of several stories set in western Ireland.

Beyond the Wide World's End

One night Timothy overhears his new step-
mother telling his father that either Timothy
must go or she will. There is only one thing to
be done – Timothy decides that he must run
away and try to find his dead mother's family
a hundred miles away on the other side of Ireland. This is the story of Timothy's adventures
with his dog Brandy and his friend Jane, both of
whom insist on coming with him on his journey.

Set in the early nineteenth century, this
exciting story for older readers is written by
Meta Mayne Reid.

More Beaver Books

We hope you have enjoyed this Beaver Book. Here are some of the other titles:

Beyond the Wide World's End Set in 1810, this is the story of how Timothy, Jane and Brandy the dog journey across Ireland in search of Timothy's dead mother's family; by Meta Mayne Reid

The Lost Island Michael unexpectedly gets a message from his father, missing for four years, and sets off on an eventful journey in search of the mysterious lost island. Set in Western Ireland, the story is written by Eilís Dillon

The Sword of the Wilderness Elizabeth Coatsworth's exciting story about a young boy captured by Indians, set at the time of the early settlement of North America

The Crocodile Based on the true story of Mary Anning, John Tully's novel for older children is set in Lyme Regis and tells of Mary's search for fossils – especially the famous 'Crocodile' – against a background of the Napoleonic Wars. With illustrations by Clifford Bayly

Twelve Great Black Cats and Other Eerie Scottish Tales Ten weird and ghostly stories with a Scottish setting; by Sorche Nic Leodhas with illustrations by Michael Jackson

The Call of the Wild The epic story of Buck, the great sledge dog in the frozen North; by Jack London

New Beavers are published every month and if you would like the *Beaver Bulletin* – which gives all the details – please send a stamped addressed envelope to

Beaver Bulletin
The Hamlyn Group
Astronaut House
Feltham
Middlesex TW14 9AR

345408